"What kind of kinky game is this?" Blake asked teasingly

Normally he wasn't into playing games with women, but Tess made him do a lot of things he didn't normally do.

"Actually, you started this round. It's still your turn," Tess reminded Blake, their bodies bathed in the shimmering candlelight of her bedroom.

"Jeez, are you always this bossy?" he quipped as he unzipped his pants. "Remember these?" Blake asked, standing opposite her in only his boxers.

Tess focused on the black boxers with little red kisses. "Did you wear those for me?"

"Yes. And I'm hoping you'll wear that silky white nightgown so that I can take it off you with my teeth. But now I'm pretty sure it's your turn."

With agonizing slowness Tess unhooked her bra and drew the straps down her arms.

Blake was hungry for her, desperate to touch her soft skin. A groan slipped from his throat.

"Is that a *good* groan or a bad groan?" Tess asked, smiling still.

Blake smiled right back. "Honey, that's an I've-died-and-gone-to-heaven groan."

Dear Reader,

Who can resist a charming man? I sure can't, and that's why I really like Blake Sutherland, the hero of *Tempting Tess*. What's great about Blake is that not only is he charming, he's also smart, witty and dependable. The last quality is what finally gets to Tess Denison. She's had her share of unreliable men. Charm goes only so far.

Of course, there are one or two other things about Blake that Tess finds tempting. Like the way he makes her laugh. And the way he listens to her concerns. Oh yeah, and the way he brings out her wild side.

As for me? I fell for his grin!

I hope you have as much fun reading Blake and Tess's story as I did writing it.

All the best,

Liz Jarrett

Books by Liz Jarrett

HARLEQUIN DUETS
20—DARN NEAR PERFECT

TEMPTING TESS
Liz Jarrett

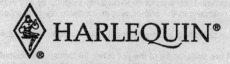

HARLEQUIN®

TORONTO • NEW YORK • LONDON
AMSTERDAM • PARIS • SYDNEY • HAMBURG
STOCKHOLM • ATHENS • TOKYO • MILAN • MADRID
PRAGUE • WARSAW • BUDAPEST • AUCKLAND

With heartfelt thanks to these special ladies:
Mary Thompson, my mom
Kathryn Lye, my editor
Nancy Yost, my agent
And Shanna Swendson (Samantha Carter), fellow writer
What can I say? You're the best!

ISBN 0-373-25927-1

TEMPTING TESS

Copyright © 2001 by Mary E. Lounsbury.

1

TESS DENISON rapped on the wooden door of Blake's apartment, tension coiling within her. Where was he? Surely he'd made it back from Cincinnati by now. But so far, he hadn't answered his phone all morning, and it looked as if he wasn't going to answer his door either.

Tess groaned and felt defeated. Men. They drove her crazy. Blake Sutherland more so than most.

"Come on, come on," she muttered, knocking again. She didn't have time for this. She'd already lost more than twenty minutes fighting Chicago traffic to get from the office to Blake's apartment. If she and Blake were going to make it back to work in time to meet their new client, she needed to find him right away.

She was about to knock one last time when the door flew open, and she found herself confronted by a broad expanse of naked, male chest.

She snatched her hand back just before it made contact, but despite herself, she gave in to temptation and stared. Sculptured tan muscles dusted with dark hair made her hands want to explore more of him. She knew deep within her that Blake's skin would be hot to the touch, searing even the most sensible woman, enticing her to do things she instinctively should avoid.

But being sensible didn't seem to be Tess's strong suit this morning. Despite her resolve to stop gawking, her gaze meandered, following the trail of chest hair as it narrowed across his taut stomach and disappeared into his low-slung jeans. The breath caught in her throat when she noticed the top button had been left undone, no doubt because he'd pulled on his jeans in a hurry.

"Glad I'm entertaining you, Tess."

At Blake's mocking words, Tess pulled her attention away from his practically indecent appearance and looked at his face. His thick black hair was mussed, attesting to the fact that she'd gotten him out of bed.

That was rich. She was probably the first woman to deliberately get him *out* of bed. Most of the women who stopped by the office made it more than clear that their main goal was to get Blake *into* bed. At the thought, her gaze skittered to his chest again and lower, to those jeans barely hanging on to his hips.

"Earth to Tess. Hello," Blake said.

She blinked, then frowned at him. His blue eyes sparkled with devilment. He knew exactly what she was thinking, and he found it funny.

Typical.

"I've been trying to reach you all morning." She forced herself to keep her gaze firmly focused on his face, which wasn't much safer. Blake Sutherland was without question the best-looking man she'd ever met. That was bad enough, but making things oh-so-much-worse was that he oozed sex. It clung to him, and no matter how much she tried, Tess couldn't look at him without thinking about hot nights and satin sheets.

Sheesh.

"My flight got in late last night, so I turned off the ringer on the phone." He ran his hand across his unshaven jaw, then yawned. "What do you want?"

Tess reminded herself again to keep to the matter at hand before she could even begin to think of a sexy, provocative, yet inappropriate response to his question.

"We have a prospective client. She called yesterday and wants to stop by and meet us at eleven." Looking at her watch, Tess added, "Which is only a little over an hour from now. We need to hurry."

At the mention of a new client, she successfully snagged Blake's attention. He shoved open the door to his apartment and waved Tess inside.

"Who's the client?" he asked, shutting the door after she entered the foyer.

Tess walked slowly into his living room, uncertain what she'd find. But there were no naked women hanging from chandeliers, no velvet paintings of Kama Sutra positions, no whips and chains scattered across the parquet floor.

Actually, the room was tastefully decorated, with cream leather furniture and gleaming mahogany tables.

"I picked up all the bras and thongs before I answered the door," Blake murmured near her ear, making Tess jump.

"Cute." She treated him to her best glare, but he only

laughed. The man made her so mad, especially when he seemed to read her mind like he'd just done.

Darn it, this was her half brother's fault. She'd been perfectly happy working as an accountant before Jason had convinced her to start an advertising agency with him and his old college roommate, Blake. Okay, so maybe perfectly happy was a small exaggeration. The huge company where she'd worked had treated her more like a piece of office equipment than a person, but still, she'd been surrounded by professionals.

Now she hung out with lunatics. Jason had insisted she'd hardly ever have to deal with Blake. The two men would be the creative team. She would handle the business side of things. And seldom the twain would meet. Hunky-dory, right?

Dummy that she was, she'd believed Jason. But now, not quite five months later, he'd taken off to find himself, leaving her stuck running the business with Blake.

The man rattled her. Like so many men she knew, Blake used his good looks to coast through life. If things weren't going his way, he'd flash a dazzling grin, murmur a few sweet-sounding words, and the world dropped into his lap. She'd been raised by a man like that. Her half brother was a man like that.

Blake Sutherland was just like them. Charming. And as she'd learned the hard way, you can't trust a charming man. When push came to shove, they'd desert you without a backward glance. That left her with one heck of a problem. She had to work with Blake if D&S Advertising was going to survive. But he made her nervous. He made her jumpy.

And despite her best resolve, he made her think about sex.

Moving farther into the living room, she sat stiffly on one of the soft leather chairs. "Do you want to hear about the client or not?"

He flopped on the matching leather sofa and flashed her a lopsided grin. "Oh, I want to hear, all right. You woke me up from a killer dream for this, so I definitely want to hear."

Tess ignored his comment, not wanting to even guess what a man like him considered a killer dream. "Debra Tomlin from Desire Perfume called me. Now that her father has retired, she wants to attract new customers, specifically younger males."

Blake arched one dark brow. "With what?"

"They have a new cologne for men," she explained, trying to keep her mind focused on the conversation and off the image of Blake lying on the couch half dressed. "So far, she doesn't like the ideas presented by their current agency. She saw the ads you did for Grant Office Supplies and Carla's Cookies and thought D&S might be able to help her company."

"Really?"

Tess knew he wasn't challenging her, but honesty forced her to blurt, "Oh, all right, she also saw the Neat and Tidy Cleaner ads and liked them."

The grin on his face widened. "Oh yeah? She liked the Neat and Tidy ads?"

"So she said." Tess picked an imaginary bit of lint off her skirt, not wanting to discuss this. Blake's racy ad campaign for Neat and Tidy Cleaner was a bone of contention between them. Or it had been, until the ads had become a big success.

Still, she firmly disagreed with his approach. His print ad featured a couple sitting on the kitchen floor kissing. Although the picture was perfectly respectable, anyone with a pulse could tell the couple was about to make love. The caption read *Aren't you glad the floor is really clean?*

"So Debra's from Desire Perfume." Blake gave Tess a long look that made her heart race. "They make Cutie Pie perfume, right? Their ads have those skinny models saying things about destiny and fate."

"Yes. That's the company. Anyway, Debra doesn't like those ads."

Blake chuckled. "I can understand why not. Weird way to advertise a perfume named Cutie Pie."

Tess ignored how the deep rumble of his laughter made little fingers of excitement dance across her skin. How in the world was it possible to be so sexually attracted to a man you didn't like? Could she be any more stupid? She knew all too well what happened to women who fell for good-looking, smooth-talking men like Blake. But stupid or not, she couldn't seem to stop the way her body reacted to him.

"You're drifting on me again, Tess. I asked what does she want from us?"

She yanked her mind back to business, took a calming breath, then said, "Their new men's cologne is aimed at the eighteen to twenty-five group. Debra said she felt we could reach those consumers."

"Sounds like fun." Blake stood and stretched, the

movement making his jeans slip even lower on his hips. Tess swallowed past the tightness in her throat. When she looked again at his face, he wore that knowing grin of his. "Well, I guess I'd better get dressed so we're not late for the meeting."

"Um, yeah," was the best she could manage.

"Did she tell you what this cologne is called? Maybe I can come up with some ideas while I shower."

Tess felt a flush creep across her face, but she congratulated herself for not breaking eye contact with him. "Loverboy."

His grin widened. "Loverboy?"

Tess stood and draped the strap of her purse over her shoulder. "Yes. I figured *you'd* have no problem thinking of an effective media campaign."

"Now, Tess, you wouldn't happen to be insulting me, would you?"

His smug expression made it more than clear he knew she'd insulted him. Naturally, she wasn't about to admit that, though.

"I'm completely sincere," she lied, ignoring the flutter in her pulse.

"Remind me to play Liar's Poker with you some day. Everything you're thinking shows up clearly on your face."

"At least I think," she blurted, then covered her mouth with her hand. Drat. Why did she let him get to her this way? "I'm sorry. My comment was rude and uncalled for."

He laughed and shook his head. "Whenever it starts to get interesting, you back off."

She wasn't certain what he meant by *interesting*, but figuring now would be a good time to escape, she said, "I have to get going."

She didn't wait for his response. She simply headed out the door, knowing eventually he'd appear in the office looking respectable. Sexy as sin, of course, but respectable. And if Debra Tomlin weren't over eighty, she'd end up under Blake's spell within ten minutes.

As Tess walked down the corridor toward the elevator, she heard a door open behind her. She didn't need to turn around to know Blake was standing in his apartment doorway, watching her leave. She told herself not to get nervous, but for the briefest of seconds, she wasn't certain she remembered how to walk.

"Hey, Tess," Blake hollered.

She didn't want to turn around, but when he yelled again, she gave up. "What?" she demanded, spinning to face him, bracing herself for whatever innuendo-laden comment he was about to make.

For several seconds, he merely looked at her, making her crazy. She shifted her weight from one conservative pump to the other and smoothed her hands down the sides of her blue wool suit jacket. "What?" she asked again.

"Thanks for getting us this chance with Desire Perfume," was all he said.

Tess stared at him, uncertain how to respond. He did seem to be sincerely thanking her. Ah, double-drat. He made her feel even guiltier for acting like such a shrew.

"Sure. And, um, sorry about the loverboy crack," she felt compelled to say.

Blake gave her another lazy grin. "You're not sorry at all."

He leaned against his doorjamb looking like pure sex poured into blue jeans. Tess debated about what to say. He was right. Truthfully, she wasn't sorry about her comment. If ever there was a man who could sell cologne named Loverboy, it was Blake Sutherland.

In the end, she simply said, "Have it your way. See you in the office in thirty minutes."

As she stepped into the elevator, she looked down the hallway. Blake still watched her.

"Hey, Tess," he yelled.

She frowned and stopped the elevator door from shutting by holding it open with her hand. "What now?"

"It will probably be closer to an hour before I get to the office. It's going to take me a long time to get all the naked women out of my bedroom."

With a groan, Tess let go of the door. As it slid shut, she heard Blake's laughter drifting down the hall.

There were times when she hated the man.

"MY MAIN GOAL for the Loverboy advertisements is to get young women to buy the cologne for the men in their lives," Debra Tomlin said, her gaze riveted on Blake, who sat across the conference table from her. "I want them to associate our cologne with a man who is fun and smart and above all...*sexy*."

She said the last word with a meaningful half smile that Blake knew was entirely for his benefit. Debra Tomlin was coming on to him. Big time. Right in the middle of the meeting. And it was really bothering Tess. Out of the corner of his eye, Blake could see his partner squirming in her chair, disapproval practically oozing off her.

But he couldn't worry about Tess right now. He needed to convince Debra that D&S Advertising could deliver the ad campaign she wanted while at the same time make it clear that he wasn't part of any deal they brokered.

"Any reason why it has to be just one guy?" he asked Debra.

The older woman studied him carefully; her face didn't give a hint of what she was thinking. She raised her hand to the side of her face and her long nails lightly touched her chin-length blond hair. "What do you have in mind?"

Blake resisted the impulse to smile. He had her. He could feel it. "You could do a series of print ads featuring Loverboy models from different cities across the country. The caption would be something like: Wherever you go, there's a Loverboy."

"Interesting," Debra said.

"We could find the models in places like New York, L.A., Boston," Annie Elliott, the agency's art director, offered. "We could use their city as a background."

"Maybe even work it into the copy," offered Drew Freeman, their copywriter.

Blake liked to see the other employees joining in on this initial brainstorming session. He could tell Debra enjoyed the attention. Everyone at D&S was involved in her campaign. It was a huge selling point when it came to dealing with someone like Debra. Someone who liked to know her business was appreciated.

And Lord knew, D&S appreciated her business.

"So we'd have a group of Loverboys," Debra said slowly, still watching Blake. "A whole collection."

Blake smiled, pleased with the way this meeting was going. It looked good. Damn good. "And if you want, we don't have to stick with traditional cities. How about Seattle and Charleston instead? That way you can appeal to a broader range of customers. Not everyone is a big city boy."

Debra returned his smile. "I like this idea. I like it a lot." With an abrupt slap to the table, she said, "Let's make it happen. What do we need to do?"

Since Tess handled the business side, she launched into a description of how the agency worked and what details needed to be mapped out, but Debra never even glanced at her. Instead, she kept looking at Blake.

He was used to the attention. Women had been looking at him like that since he'd been fifteen. At that age, that kind of look had meant he was about to score. Even then he'd followed two strict rules—always practice safe sex and try not to break anyone's heart. Now that he was thirty, he had one more rule—never fool around with a client. Ever.

Debra Tomlin was just going to have to accept that fact.

"This is what I want," Debra said, leaning toward him. The small conference room table kept some distance between them, but not much. "I want you to put these ads together as quickly as possible. If the print ads fly, then we'll tackle billboards and TV."

"Perhaps we should take a moment to discuss the details of this agreement," Tess said. "We can do a few mock-ups. If you like those, I can work up a contract in a few days, and then we can—"

Debra silenced Tess with a wave of her hand, then flashed another cat-like smile at him. "Whatever. My assistant will be in touch with you later today. But Blake, you're definitely the man I want on my campaign. Most *definitely*."

Blake frowned at her not-so-subtle message. "All of us at D&S work together as a team, Debra."

With a shrug of her elegantly clad shoulders, she said, "Whatever." She smiled again and added, "You know, Blake, you're exactly the sort of man we want for Loverboy."

He didn't know where she was going with this, but he wanted to stop it now. "I'm too old for your demographics," he pointed out.

"I think you're the perfect loverboy," she said, still studying him. "Perfect."

From across the room, Blake heard Tess suck in a tight breath. This situation was getting out of hand, but luck was with him. The door of the conference room opened and their very pregnant secretary, Molly Renfro, signaled to Tess.

"Excuse me," Tess said stiffly as she stood and headed toward the door.

Debra barely glanced at Drew and Annie as she

asked, "Give me a couple of minutes with your boss, okay?"

Tess stopped walking and turned to look at Blake. Drew and Annie stared at him, too, obviously uncertain what to do. Debra's request surprised Blake as much as it did the rest of them, but he nodded.

With a lot of commotion, Drew and Annie collected their things and joined Tess. Blake watched all three leave, but he focused mostly on Tess. She was really upset. It was obvious from the way she walked, her back absolutely straight. She looked like a schoolmarm with her shapeless blue suit, her hair woven into a bun-like thing on the back of her head, and disapproval dripping off her.

His gaze dropped to her legs, or what little he could see peeking out from the bottom of her skirt. Tess had nice calves. Great calves, actually. He wondered not for the first time what else she hid under her boxy suits. He was hard up if he was thinking about what Tess looked like naked. But from time to time, the thought did cross his mind.

But now, he had a different dilemma to deal with. As soon as the door shut and they were alone, he returned his attention to Debra. "Thanks, but my loverboy days are behind me."

Debra simply smiled that cat-smile again. "If you say so."

"I also think there's something I should explain. I don't mix business with pleasure. Hope that won't be a problem."

Of all the reactions he expected, one wasn't for Debra to laugh. But that's what she did. "Whatever. No big deal."

That had been easy. "Not that under different circumstances I wouldn't—"

"How sweet of you to say so." She glanced at her watch. "I guess we're through here."

Damn. Maybe she hadn't taken the rejection as well as he'd thought. Had he blown the deal? Was she going to walk?

"Listen, Debra, I—"

She stood and gave him a knowing smile. "Relax. You have the account."

He stood, too, relief flowing through his veins. "Just like that?"

"Just like that. I've done my research. I know the kind of work you did at Markland and Jacobs. And I like what you've done since starting D&S, especially the ads for Neat and Tidy Cleaner. I believe in you. Your people and my people can work out the specifics." She paused for a second, then added, "And for the record, it's your loss."

He laughed, liking a woman who took rejection with such flair. "I'm absolutely certain of that."

Blake walked Debra out of the conference room and to the reception area. After making arrangements to meet again, he thanked her for the contract and shook her hand.

Once Debra left, Blake wandered back down the hallway, looking for Tess and ignoring the questioning looks Annie and Drew gave him. Right now, he wanted to talk to Tess. She'd be thrilled when he told her the good news.

He found her in her office talking on the phone. When she saw him, she quickly ended the call.

"Sorry. That was the Neat and Tidy folks on the phone. They want to move their ads to TV." She looked beyond him, then returned her gaze to his face. From out of nowhere it occurred to Blake that her hazel eyes were unusual. Unique. Pretty. Really pretty. They were so light that at times, like when she was upset, they appeared almost silver. Come to think of it, they looked pretty damn silver right now.

"What happened? Where is Ms. Tomlin?"

"Debra had to go." When Tess started to protest, he quickly told her, "Cool off. She gave us the account."

That sucked the fury right out of her. Blake walked across the room and dropped into the chair facing her desk. "Close your mouth, Tess."

She gave him that tight-lipped, old-lady frown of hers and he chuckled.

"My mouth wasn't open, and I can't believe the way Debra flirted with you. Talk about being completely unprofessional. She doesn't really think that just because she gave us her account, that you'll..." He saw something like fear cross Tess's face. "You wouldn't, I mean you didn't...do anything. Did you?"

Blake wasn't certain whether to be insulted or amused. Insulted won out. "Calm down. I didn't have sex with her on the conference room table. In fact, I made it clear I wasn't going to have sex with her any-where, anytime." The more he thought about Tess's reaction, the more it bothered him. Sure, they hadn't been working together long, but come on? She was his partner. She needed to have more faith in him.

"You know, I do have more talents than just those involving sex," he said slowly, irritation rising in him. He rarely got mad, but Tess pushed the right buttons. Her opinion was not justified—just because the first time they'd met, he'd gone out on not one but two dates the previous evening. He'd only been nineteen and finally had a small taste of freedom. So sue him.

"I didn't say a word," she said primly.

"Yeah, you did. With that look you're always giving me."

"What look? I didn't give you any kind of look."

"Yeah, you did."

She tilted her chin. "Well, if I'm giving you looks, perhaps you deserve them. Debra certainly got the impression that you two had something private to discuss."

Okay. That was it. Blake stood and circled her desk until he faced her. She started to rise also, but he leaned down and placed his hands on the arms of her chair. He hadn't intended on confronting Tess like this, but maybe it was about time. They needed to clear the air, and since he was there he might as well do it now.

Tess leaned away from him. "Move," she said firmly.

"In a minute. I want to say something without you running away. I don't like that Jason disappeared on us any more than you do, Tess. I'm stuck and I know you are, too. I left a good job and put my savings into this business just like you did. And I want to make D&S succeed."

Tess looked more startled than annoyed as she sat rigidly in her chair. He drew in a deep breath and continued, "I don't care what you think I do in my personal life, but I'm good at my job. And I don't mess around with clients. You think I'm some kind of satyr, laying anything that walks by me, and I think you're a dried-up old prune who wouldn't know what to do with a man if one dropped naked into her lap. But none of that matters. What matters is we had better learn how to work together before we both end up bankrupt. If we can make the Loverboy campaign successful, we can get enough financing so one of us can buy the other's share of the ad agency. That will solve our problem."

Then he shoved away from her chair and headed toward the door, not waiting to see her reaction to what he'd said. He hated that she got him this crazy. He never got mad. He had no respect for people who couldn't control their emotions.

His father had always been furious. Furious at life. Anger ate at him until one day, at forty-nine, he'd died of a heart attack.

Blake refused to be like him. But no matter how hard he tried, he couldn't seem to keep from getting aggravated around Tess. He headed to his office, closing the door behind him, barely resisting the impulse to slam it. Great. Now she had yet another reason to dislike him. Just what he needed.

"Way to go, genius," he muttered to himself, dropping into his chair and swiveling until he faced the window behind his desk. Telling Tess off wouldn't help. In fact, it was a surefire way to make this situation even more miserable.

At this particular moment, Blake dearly hoped Jason ran into the Abominable Snowman on his trek through the Himalayas. It would serve him right to end up being dinner for a thousand-pound ice monster.

HE THOUGHT she was a dried-up old prune? *A prune?* Why, because she didn't sleep around? She had morals and scruples and principles. Okay, so she might be a tad reserved, but that didn't mean she was a prune.

And for his information, she most certainly would know what to do with a naked man if one dropped into her lap. Ha! She stood, intending to go to his office and tell him so, then realized how stupid she'd sound if she did.

Tess sighed and rubbed her temples. As much as she hated admitting it, he was right. She needed to stop judging him. His plan sounded perfect. She'd let him find financing and buy out her share of the business. Then she'd figure out what kind of work she'd like to do. Maybe she'd rejoin the accounting firm.

Or maybe not.

A wave of nausea roiled through her stomach. She prided herself on being fair, on always giving people the benefit of the doubt. Yet just because a few women had stopped by the office to flirt with Blake, she'd decided he was still as wild as he'd been in college.

When it came right down to it, how he lived his personal life was none of her business. All she had the right to comment on was his professional behavior, which was...fine. Thanks to the great connections he'd had at his previous agency, D&S had landed three major accounts in the last few months. Now it looked as though it was time to thank him again, since they'd also landed Desire Perfume.

No way around it. She owed Blake an apology.

Never one to shirk a responsibility, Tess forced herself to walk to Blake's office. Blake had closed his door, something he never did. Just one more sign of how angry he was.

Tess knocked on the door, but when he didn't answer, she opened the door anyway. His back was to her, and he didn't turn to face her as she entered his office.

Tess cleared her throat, then said, "If this was a movie, I'd offer you an elaborate apology, admitting that you were right and I was wrong. Then, only after I'd completely groveled, would I discover you had a knife through your chest and hadn't heard a word I'd said."

Blake swiveled his chair around until he faced her. "I shouldn't have gotten mad."

Tess tucked her hands into the pockets of her jacket. "Don't apologize. I'm glad you said what you did. I deserved it. And you're right. We need to work together to make this company succeed." She took a couple of steps closer to his desk. "Then you can buy me out."

His expression remained unreadable. "Fair enough."

"But I want something in return," she added.

She saw a glint of humor in his blue eyes, and a thawing in his demeanor. "Of course. And what do you want me to do for you?"

Tess raised her chin and met his gaze. How did he make a simple question sound like an invitation to fulfill her fantasies? "That. I want you to stop doing that."

Blake frowned. "What 'that' exactly am I supposed to stop doing?"

Refusing to let him get to her, she explained, "That male flirty thing you do."

With a chuckle, he asked, "You think I'm flirting with you?"

He sounded so surprised that Tess felt stupid, but she wouldn't back down. "Not flirting," she explained. "I think you're mocking me most of the time. You think teasing me is funny."

"No, I don't." When she continued to look at him, he laughed and said, "Okay, maybe I tease you a little."

"You tease me a lot. As you said, you think I'm a prune, and you like to ruffle my feathers."

She could tell he wanted to laugh again, but he didn't. Instead, he asked, "I really upset you? I don't mean to."

"Yes, you do, so don't pretend otherwise."

Blake stood and headed toward her, so she took a half step back, needing to keep some distance between them. When he got too close, her IQ tended to drop. "Do we have a deal?"

Blake stopped when he reached the front of his desk. His look was direct and unwavering. "I'll *try* not to tease you," he said. "But you do realize we're going to be spending the next few weeks traveling around the country looking for Loverboy models. If you go all stiff and schoolmarmy on me, I may have no choice but to tease you out of it."

They were going looking for Loverboys? Now that idea meant imminent disaster. And what exactly did he mean by that schoolmarmy crack?

"About the trips," she said. "Maybe I should stay here and run the office while you—"

He cut her off with a snort. "No way. I'm not picking the Loverboy models, you are. I'll come up with the ideas for the copy, but that's it. In fact, the only reason I'm coming is because someone needs to handle the details while you decide which guys jump-start your engine."

"I have to decide?" The thought of picking the models made her head hurt. She didn't want to do this. Not at all. "Annie could do it."

Blake shook his head. "No. Not Annie. *You* have to decide. This is your company." He leaned back against his desk. "Don't worry. You'll have fun."

Tess repressed a shudder. "No, I won't. I'll feel..."

"What?"

"I don't know, like a dirty old woman."

"Why? You're going to be offering these young men one hell of a good deal. They'll make terrific money for just standing around and looking cute. Seems easy enough to me."

Based on their newly minted truce, she tried to reason with him. "I'm not comfortable with the concept."

"The concept of interviewing handsome young men?"

There was a lot more involved than simply doing interviews and he knew it. "I'll have to judge them on their sex appeal."

With a shrug, he asked, "So why is that a problem? I'm sure any guy who can get your juices flowing is bound to be a big hit with the rest of the female population."

Tess narrowed her eyes. He'd just insulted her. She was certain of it. Hadn't he?

She put her hands on her hips. "What do you mean by that?"

His innocent expression never wavered. "Nothing. Why? What did you think I meant?" Moving toward her, he said, "Come on, Tess. This is a great assignment. Lighten up."

He stopped directly in front of her, and her pulse took off at a gallop. Blake had just revved her engine. But she wasn't about to give him the satisfaction of looking flustered.

"Tell you what," he said. "Next time a company wants us to pick six sexy young women, I'll take the assignment."

"I'm sure." Tess let out a long sigh. She knew she had no choice. They needed this account, and he was right—the young men would get paid well for modeling. She and Blake weren't going to take advantage of anyone.

But it wasn't just picking the models that bothered her. She didn't want to travel with Blake. She had enough trouble being around him in the office. He exasperated and annoyed her. He also made her heart race and her palms sweat.

To her chagrin, she wasn't any better than Debra Tomlin or the other women who lusted after him. What would it be like spending all day working with him, then going back to a hotel at night? Sooner or later, would she make a fool of herself around him, assuming of course, that she didn't kill him first?

The scenario was filled with the potential for catastrophe.

But she couldn't admit her concern to him. In a resigned tone she said, "Fine. I'll do it, but just so you know, I would rather be sawed in half at a carnival show."

A slow, easy grin appeared on his face. "Now that's what I like to see—enthusiasm. Don't worry, once we get started, you'll have a great time."

"Yeah, as long as you don't drop any of those young men naked into my lap," she muttered heading for the door.

What in the world had she gotten herself into?

2

TESS FELT like one of fifteen clowns stuffed into a compact car. The seats in coach on her flight to Dallas weren't meant to hold men the size of the two bracketing her. The one on her right was Blake, who made a sincere effort not to intrude on her personal space, but at six-two, she could tell he was more than a little cramped.

Then there was the man on her left. The word octopus described him better. Rather than trying to stay out of her personal space, his hands seemed to wander off on their own, ending up unerringly on her leg. When she'd swat at him, he'd give her a leering smile and say, "Oops. Don't know how that got there."

Tess wanted to scream.

Compounding her jangled nerves was the very real fear that nothing would go right on this trip. The staff hadn't taken nearly enough time to plan and double-check the details. Worse yet, Blake had made the arrangements with the modeling agencies, which did nothing to instill confidence in her. A million things could go wrong.

"Did you get confirmations from all of the agencies?" she asked Blake. "They know we're coming, right? Everything's set up, right?" She turned toward him as much as possible.

Blake put down his paperback and looked at her. Rather than appearing exasperated, his blue eyes sparkled with humor. "Okay. We'll go over this again if you like. Yes, Tess, everything is set. Interviews with three agencies are arranged for tomorrow. We're good to go, so stop worrying."

Tess wished she *could* stop worrying, but she simply couldn't. This was the first time she'd been involved in a project this big, and she didn't like the sensation of not being in control. Blake was calling the shots, and that flat-out made her nervous.

Not to mention how jittery she was about being in such close proximity to him for the next couple of weeks. Even now, sitting on a crowded airplane, all she could focus on was him. She couldn't help noticing he smelled like heaven, and she had this crazy, stupid desire to lean closer to him.

Instead, she leaned away, bumping the man next to her, to whom she muttered a quick apology. She forced herself to get a grip and smiled politely at Blake.

"Sorry to bother you again," she told him. "But I want everything on this trip to be perfect. So you're certain we have confirmations?"

Blake sighed loudly, then patted her hand, which was on the armrest between their seats. The brief contact didn't make her feel better. Oh, no. It made her heart do an annoying little lurch-sputter, which couldn't be good any way she looked at it.

She yanked her hand away from his, causing him to

arch one dark brow. For a second he only studied her. Then a slow, sexy smile crossed his face.

"You know, Tess, that's one of the things about you that I..."

When he hesitated, she froze, waiting for his next word. He was going to tease her. She knew it. So much for their truce.

"You what?" she asked, certain she didn't want to hear his answer but needing to know it anyway.

His smile only grew and she knew she was in for trouble. "One of the things I really like about you. That you get so excited."

The word "excited" dripped with sexual innuendo, and Tess frowned. "I do not."

Blake chuckled. "Sure you do," he said, his voice husky. "And the best part is that you make so much noise when you're excited."

Okay, that was it. He could sit there with that smug look on his face pretending he wasn't teasing her, but he darn well was. And they had an agreement to play nice.

This was *not* playing nice. She felt anger grow and twist inside her, fueled by a part of her—an almost miniscule part of her—that stupidly responded to his sex-on-satin-sheets voice and the devilish gleam in his eyes.

This trip was turning out so much worse than she'd feared. They hadn't even landed in Dallas yet, and already she wanted to simultaneously kiss and kill the man.

What were the next couple of months going to be like?

She had to get control of her emotions. She gave Blake the iciest look she could muster. But rather than subduing him, he winked at her.

Arrgh!

A bump against her back reminded her that the man with the wandering hands probably hung on their every word. Just peachy-keen. He no doubt would become even more aggressive now that he'd heard Blake say she was noisy when excited.

Tess forced herself to calm down. Getting angry didn't do any good. Blake was baiting her, and she knew it. Normally she rarely got angry and never got flustered. Only Blake seemed to pull those reactions out of her, and she wasn't too pleased about his talent at ticking her off.

But she would not get mad. She wouldn't allow herself to get mad.

Instead, she plastered on her most seductive smile. She knew it wasn't as perfect as his, but it must have been pretty good because for the briefest moment, Blake looked startled.

Ha! Let him be caught off guard for once. Turning in her seat slightly, she saw the Octopus was indeed listening closely to their conversation.

"My friend is so sweet and so brave," she confided to the stranger. "I'm proud of him."

She could feel Blake watching her, but she ignored him. Instead she kept her attention focused on the groper next to her.

"Why are you proud of him?" the man asked, sneaking a hand onto her knee.

Gritting her teeth, Tess moved his hand away. "I have notoriously bad luck with men. The first two I was involved with both died." She opened her eyes wide and gave a small gasp. "In terrible, *terrible* accidents."

The groper leaned a little away from her. "Really? But that's not your fault," he said, although he didn't look convinced.

"That's what *I* thought. I mean how could anyone possibly blame me?" After briefly glancing at Blake, who was obviously fighting a smile, she turned back to the other man. "Of course, that was before Blake's accident."

The man's face paled. "Accident?"

Tess nodded and did the little sob-gasp again. "Yes. It was terrible. He and I were just becoming..." She shrugged. "You know, acquainted, when boom, it happened."

"What?" The stranger pressed himself firmly against the window.

Tess sighed dramatically. "The industrial accident. That machine sliced off his...um..." She glanced at his lap, and the stranger slammed both hands across his groin in a protective gesture. "Well, you know."

What little color remained in the man's face drained away. "Really?" he squeaked.

"Really. We're off to see some specialists in Dallas who may be able to help." Tess could feel the burn of Blake's stare on her back. Well, it served him right. Her new partner needed to know she wasn't going to sit around and let him tease her as if she were a schoolgirl.

Deciding that ought to put a damper on both men for the rest of the flight, she figured now was a good time to go to the restroom. "If you gentlemen will excuse me, I need to powder my nose."

She stood, and the groper glanced beyond her to shoot a sympathetic look at Blake.

"Sorry to hear about your trouble," he said, shock still evident in his voice.

To give him credit, Blake didn't even try to deny what she'd said. He simply shrugged. "Thanks, but it's not the end of the world."

Blake stood so Tess could scoot by him to reach the aisle. At first she thought he wasn't going to retaliate and that maybe he'd finally gotten her not-so-subtle message that she sincerely didn't want to be teased. But she should have known better. When she was even with Blake, his arm snaked around her waist, and he pulled her close.

With his attention fully focused on the other man, Blake said, "I'm learning to cope. And thankfully for Tess here, I still have my tongue."

"DO YOU WANT me to take off my shirt?" the young man asked.

Blake set a stack of photos down on the table and glanced up at the model. Like all the countless other guys who had stopped by today, this one was trying to look sexy. With a frown, Blake pointed at Tess. "I definitely don't, but she'll want you to."

The kid nodded and headed across the hotel meeting room to where Tess had squashed herself into a corner. Blake grinned as he watched yet another picture perfect boy-stud strut across the room and start to flirt with Tess. She looked like a virgin about to be thrown into a volcano—horrified. No doubt about it. She hated interviewing the male models. Absolutely hated it.

He bit back a smile. He didn't have any sympathy for her after that stunt on the plane yesterday. An industrial accident? He'd give her this—she was creative. But she also had an annoying streak down her back a mile wide. When she'd returned from the restroom, she'd remained noticeably silent the rest of the flight. As soon as they had landed, she'd grabbed her luggage and told him she'd meet him at the hotel later.

But she hadn't. She'd disappeared into a taxi and he hadn't seen her again until he'd walked into this conference room at nine this morning. She'd given him that frosty look she specialized in and had immediately gotten down to business. He had no idea when she'd arrived at the hotel, but he did know her room was on a different floor from his. Since the hotel was half empty, he had to assume the placement was intentional. What was she afraid of? That he'd sleepwalk?

As immature as it sounded, Tess ignoring him irked Blake. He hated the silent treatment. Always had. Definitely always would.

Blake glanced over at Tess and the model, and then grinned when the young man pulled his shirt off and posed for Tess. She scooted her chair even farther into the corner, almost if she were afraid of the kid.

Damn, she really was a prune. She couldn't even bring herself to relax and enjoy this assignment. How hard could it be for a red-blooded woman to look at handsome young men all day? But Tess acted as if she were being roasted alive.

Blake watched as she pulled herself together somewhat and gave the model her ice-queen stare. Within seconds, the kid had his shirt back on and sat politely in the chair in front of Tess. Having experienced that look of hers more often than he cared to admit, Blake could testify it packed a wallop. It pulled a man back in line within microseconds.

All things considered, he wished he could simply buy Tess's share of the business right now, and they could go their separate ways. But unfortunately, like her, he'd sunk substantial savings into this company. He'd be damned if he would walk away from that investment. His finances weren't in any shape to stand that kind of loss, especially not with his sister's grad school tuition coming due in another few weeks.

Unlike Tess and her brother, he hadn't inherited a trust fund. He'd earned his money by working hard even as a kid. Slowly, over the years, those pennies had added up to dollars, but it never seemed to be enough. His mom and younger sister, Lisa, still counted on him to help pay the bills. That was why he'd jumped at the chance when Jason suggested starting their own agency. For eight years, Blake had slaved away at Markland and Jacobs, the big ad firm he'd joined right out of college. He was certain he had a shot at making partner. But it hadn't happened, so opening his own agency seemed like the next best way to make some serious cash.

He'd worked too hard for this business to fail, and it would fail if they lost the Desire Perfume account. Tess needed to pick the first Loverboy model soon so that Debra's faith in them didn't waver.

After they finished this account, though, they'd both be happy. Once he got all the financing together, he could buy out Tess. She didn't like the business and she sure as hell didn't like him. He didn't have to be a mind reader to know the woman couldn't wait to get away from him.

It had to be a first. Not that he was conceited, but usually women liked him. A lot. He had to chase them off sometimes. But not Tess. Despite the covert looks she gave him now and again, he knew she didn't like him. And that wasn't his idea of a successful partnership.

Noting that the interview in the corner was winding down, Blake stood and wandered over to where Tess and the model faced each other with more than a little wariness.

"I appreciate you stopping by, and we have your picture," Tess indifferently told the blond, blue-eyed young man.

The kid looked up at him, clearly baffled. Blake shrugged. Damned if he knew what she was looking for. This kid, like all the others, seemed fine to him.

But Tess obviously remained unaffected.

After shaking hands, the model left, and Blake settled into the now empty chair facing Tess.

"So tell me, what was wrong with him?" he asked.

Tess glanced around the room, finding all sorts of things to distract her from looking directly at him.

"I don't think he's what we want," she said vaguely.

"Why not? Too tall? Too short? Not handsome enough? Tess, we're only in Dallas for another day. You need to pick someone. You've spent the entire day talking to good-looking guys. One of them must have turned you on."

At that remark, she finally made eye contact with him. "You have such a way with words."

Blake ran his hands through his hair. This was going to be a long trip if Tess didn't lighten up. "Okay, let me try again. Weren't you attracted to any of them?"

Tess groaned and shook her head. "I'm sorry, but I wasn't. Well, certainly not enough to buy anything they were selling."

He'd caught Tess giving him looks before, so he'd always assumed she was into guys, but hell, maybe he was wrong. He knew he was way off base with the question he was about to ask, but he had to ask it anyway. "You do like guys, right?"

"Excuse me?"

Okay, he had his answer. "Never mind."

She looked flustered but her voice was steady when she said, "No. No. You're right. It's a legitimate question. And yes, I do like men. Very much. I simply didn't like any of those models."

So now they were getting somewhere. Or maybe not.

"Care explaining what it is you do find attractive in a guy if none of those models fit the bill?"

When she met and held his gaze, Blake found it impossible to look away. Tess looked as confused as he felt. She also looked anxious, and tired, and...cute, with her face flushed and her hair starting to escape that awful bun she wore.

Blake blinked. *Cute?* He thought Tess was cute? Where'd that idea come from? He must really be tired.

"I know you're upset with me, and I don't blame you," she said. "I also realize I can't even explain why those models don't work for me, but they don't. I'm absolutely positive choosing any of the young men we saw today would be a big mistake."

The blush on her face had faded only a little, distracting Blake for a second from the bright conviction in her eyes. Whatever the reason, Tess was certain about this.

And as her partner, he had to accept her answer. She deserved his respect, if for no other reason than she'd hung in with him even after her half brother had deserted the firm.

"Okay, fine," he said. "We'll see if anyone special comes along tomorrow."

While standing, he gathered the glossy photos the models had left behind, then offered them to Tess. "Just in case you want to refresh your memory tonight."

She accepted the pictures reluctantly. "I won't change my mind."

"Fine. Want to grab some dinner, then?"

Tess vehemently shook her head. "I can't. Not tonight. I'm going to order room service because I have too many things to catch up on."

"What things?"

"Stuff. Reading. You know."

No, he didn't know, but he wasn't going to push it. If Tess didn't want to eat dinner with him, then fine. He'd eat by himself. No big deal.

Except if it was no big deal, then why did he feel disappointed?

Either way, it didn't matter. He pushed the chair he'd been sitting in under the table near her, then gave her a wave.

"See you tomorrow," he said, heading for the door. He knew she was watching him leave, and the crazy part was he wanted to turn around and look at her again.

But, of course, he didn't. He kept walking, deciding he needed this time alone tonight to see if he could figure out why he was suddenly losing his mind. And he was losing his mind. That was a given.

Why else would Tess be getting to him this way?

TESS PACED her hotel bedroom, anxiety making her stomach ache. Something was wrong. Dead wrong. And she couldn't sleep until she found an answer to the million-dollar question: Why *hadn't* any of those extremely good-looking and well-built young men turned her on?

They'd been some of the handsomest men she'd ever met, each one certainly every bit as handsome as Blake. And yet they all had left her cold, while one crooked smile from Blake was all it took for her common sense to go into hibernation. Around him, all she could think about was sex.

Worse than that, he made her want to have sex. With him.

Right now.

Sheesh. She sat on the side of the bed, tired and frustrated in more ways than one. Here she was, responsible for picking the perfect Loverboy model, and all she could think about was Blake. If she didn't get a grip on herself, they could lose this account as quickly as they'd gotten it.

Tomorrow, whether she liked it or not, she had to pick a Dallas candidate for the ads. Choosing that person would be a lot easier if she could figure out why Blake got her hot and those handsome models left her cold. This attraction she reluctantly felt for her partner had nothing to do with admiration and everything to do with hormones. She wasn't falling for Blake, she just wanted him.

In shockingly wild and wicked ways.

Forcing herself to stay on task, she slowly turned the problem over in her mind. What was the difference? Why did Blake get to her and the models didn't?

The answer hit her like a slap in the face. Blake was real. He wasn't a picture-perfect guy who spent all of his time fussing about his looks. If fact, as far as she could tell, Blake spent absolutely no time fussing about his looks. And yet he still made her knees go weak and her mind wander in dangerous directions.

He was natural. A real man, not a model. Someone

true. Blake was sexy not because he was handsome, but because he was smart, and confident, and funny.

Tess smiled, thrilled that she'd found the solution. Now she'd be able to find the perfect Loverboy spokesmen without any trouble. Grabbing the phone on the nightstand, she dialed Blake's room, wanting to tell him her idea.

"Hmmph," he muttered into the phone.

"Blake. Tess. Sorry to call so late, but I've figured out the problem."

There was a long pause, then Blake's sleepy voice rumbled deep and husky over the phone line. "Tess, it's the middle of the night. You don't call someone this late unless there's an emergency or you want to have phone sex. So which is it?"

His voice danced across her skin like a caress. Tess had to stop herself from hanging up the phone. She wasn't going to let Blake distract her.

"Ha, ha. Now here's what I've figured out. The reason those young men didn't attract me today was because they were models."

With a resigned groan, Blake said, "Run that by me again."

"They were perfect. Perfect bodies. Perfect faces. Perfect teeth."

He chuckled. "Ah. So you like men who have lots of flaws, is that it?"

In a way, he was right. "Not *lots* of flaws, but real. And I think that's what will make this ad campaign successful. Let's take average guys, nice looking, but not model types. Guys who are smart, who are com-

fortable with who they are. We'll photograph them as
we find them, then maybe give them just a tad of polish
by doing 'after' shots where they have a new haircut
and a new wardrobe. The selling point then is that any
man can be a Loverboy, someone smart and sexy. Men
will want to buy Loverboy cologne because anyone can
be transformed. Women will want to buy the cologne
for the men in their lives. So, what do you think?''

Tess held her breath while she waited for his reaction. When he still hadn't said anything after what
seemed like an eternity to her, she asked, ''Well?''

''I like it, but before we discuss it any further, tell me
what you're wearing.''

She groaned. ''I'm not doing this, Blake, so let's stick
to business.''

''This is business. Tell me what you're wearing.''

This was business like she was the queen of Mars,
but she knew he wouldn't let the joke go until he was
darn well ready. Plus, that annoying, miniscule part of
her that kept getting her into trouble found the idea of
flirting with Blake over the phone in the middle of the
night exciting.

She sighed, more for his benefit than for hers. ''All
right. We'll play your little game. I'm wearing a white
cotton nightgown.''

His laugh was more of a hoot. ''I knew it.''

Now she was insulted, because his simple ''I knew
it'' meant that he figured naturally a dried-up prune
would wear a cotton nightgown. Despite herself, she
added, ''It's not what you think at all. The nightgown is

very pretty, long with a bell skirt and bluebonnets sprinkled across the yoke."

"The yoke? What's a yoke? And if it's anything like garters, then I take back my laugh."

"You are so twelve," she said with a huff. Why in the world had she played along with this game? "Anyway, let's talk about Loverboy."

"Not yet. You still haven't told me what a yoke is."

And if she had any sense, she wouldn't tell him. Unfortunately, she seemed to have left her common sense at home, because the next thing she knew, she blurted, "The yoke is the top part of the gown, the bodice."

"Now there's a word I recognize."

Of course he did. She knew he was a man who had seen his fair share of bodices over the years. Feeling more than a little deflated now, Tess decided it was past time to end the game.

"Let's talk about Loverboy tomorrow when you're focused on the account."

"I like your idea," he said, laughter tinting his voice. "But I've become distracted. Now all I can think about are white gowns and bodices."

Tess was riled by his teasing. "Do you have to joke all the time? Can't you ever just have a normal conversation with me?"

"Apparently not any more than you can have a normal conversation with me."

He had her there. She didn't have normal conversations with him. Not really. Most of the time, he aggravated her so much that she could barely talk. And when he wasn't aggravating her, he was...distracting her in other ways.

"We can talk some more tomorrow," she said, prepared to hang up and end this nonsense.

"Okay. If that's what you want."

But it wasn't what she wanted. Not really. She wanted Blake to take her seriously, for once see her as something more than an old, stodgy prune. Suddenly, unexpectedly, an impish notion reared up inside her because before she knew what she was doing she blurted, "But you still need to tell me what you're wearing."

Yikes. Where had that come from? Tess held her breath at her own outrageousness, but she couldn't help it. He'd started this game, and now she was curious.

"Wow, Tess, I'm surprised at you." He chuckled again, but there was something in his voice that didn't reflect his usual teasing tone. Underneath she could tell he was actually enjoying this, too. That knowledge gave her a little thrill and made it easy to continue.

"Fair is fair, Mr. Sutherland. So fess up. What are you wearing?" She braced herself, knowing he was going to say nothing.

"Okay. I'm wearing boxers."

That surprised her. She'd figured him for a nothing-but-a-smile kind of guy.

"Really? Boxers?" In some bizarre way, she felt disappointed, which was stupid. Just like flirting with Blake was stupid. "Well, thanks for telling me. I guess I'll see you in the morning."

"Tess."

That was all he said, just her name. But the way he said it made her temperature rise.

"Um, yes?" She curled her fingers against the cool sheets on her bed. She could clearly imagine him sitting up in his own bed, wearing only boxer shorts, looking like sin with mischief dancing in his eyes and a half grin on his sexy mouth.

Oh, my.

"Tess, don't you want to know what my boxers look like?"

Did she want to know? Could her heart stand the strain?

"That's not really necessary," she answered, more out of self-preservation than sincerity. Because, as much as she hated herself for wanting to know, she wanted to know. But she was a coward and she knew it.

"Now, don't be that way," he teased in that deep velvet voice of his. "You want to know, don't you? You're just too shy to ask."

He was playing with her, purposely trying to fluster her. Obviously, women who wore cotton nightgowns with bluebonnets scattered across the yoke weren't taken seriously by Blake. He certainly didn't take *her* seriously.

But she wanted him to, so she made sure her voice was barely above a whisper when she said, "Yes, Blake, I want to know."

After a noticeable pause, that she hoped was the result of her sexy siren's voice, Blake finally said, "The boxers are black with little red kisses all over."

Tess's heartbeat flitter-fluttered, and she felt her breath catch in her throat. Little kisses all over? The image that quickly flashed through her mind did nothing to settle her heart rate or restore her breathing.

"Have sweet dreams, Tess," Blake murmured. Then he hung up.

With a sigh, Tess replaced the handset. She wasn't certain her dreams would be sweet, but she was absolutely positive they'd be filled with little red kisses.

3

BLAKE GLANCED UP from his breakfast menu and studied Tess across the table. She looked flustered this morning. And tired. That was good. He was glad he wasn't the only one to lose sleep last night after their phone call ended. He still couldn't believe the way he had flirted with her, but what he really couldn't believe was that she'd flirted back. Whether she'd meant to or not.

Thus, he was tired this morning. Tired and feeling like a fool. Flirting with Tess was a bad idea. Very bad. Without even breaking into a mental sweat, he could think of all sorts of things that could go wrong if they headed down that path. For starters, he never got involved with women who expected anything more than a short-term fling. He didn't do relationships. Ever. He was already drowning in responsibilities, and besides, love flat-out didn't last.

Not that Tess would be interested in a relationship with him. Despite last night's phone flirtation, she made it clear on a daily basis that she didn't like him. She expected him to mess up, and Blake's experience had taught him sooner or later, he probably would. At least he would as far as Tess was concerned. She had impossibly high standards of behavior. Maybe that rigid streak of hers was a result of having grown up in a family of screw-ups. According to Jason, their mutual father was always starting things, then abandoning them whenever the going got tough. His marriages. His businesses. His charm was the only reason he wasn't destitute. Blake had met the guy once, and he was a coaster—someone who drifted through life without working too hard at anything.

But Blake did work hard, and he didn't bail at the first sign of bad weather. Tess would figure that out sooner or later. In the meantime he needed to stop thinking of her as anything more than his straight-laced partner. Who cared if she slept in a white nightgown with tiny flowers? And what difference did it make that her hair looked nice this morning? She'd obviously been in a rush and hadn't twisted it into her usual masochistic bun. Instead, her light brown hair was pulled back into a simple ponytail. The strands looked soft. Sensual.

Damn. He needed his head examined.

Blake took a long sip of black coffee, then asked, "Any idea where we can find this normal guy you want for the ad campaign? We can't simply drive around town until we find someone. And what if the guy you pick turns out to have a criminal record or something?"

Tess looked up from her own menu. "We'll have the man's background checked. But we would've needed to do that even if we'd gone with one of the models." Her gaze narrowed as she regarded him. "Just because someone is handsome doesn't mean he's a nice guy."

Ouch. Blake couldn't resist smiling at her obvious dig. "That was about as subtle as a slap with a two-by-four, Tess."

"Why would you think I'm talking about you?"

Ah, now this was the Tess he knew and understood. The Tess who wouldn't go easy on him if he were dangling at the end of a lynching rope. "Because you are and we both know it. You're upset about the phone sex thing."

"Shh." Tess's gaze darted around the restaurant, and when it became clear no one had heard him, she finally looked back at Blake. "It wasn't phone sex."

"Fine. Phone foreplay, then."

A rose-colored tint slowly crept up her face, finally flooding her neck and cheeks. "Can we please stay focused? I agree we need a plan for finding the perfect candidate. If I'd thought of this before we'd gotten to Dallas, we could have made arrangements with one of the local colleges to recruit."

Blake almost pointed out to her that she hadn't disputed his earlier claim about the call being foreplay. So she, too, thought things had gotten a little hotter than expected last night. It hadn't been just kidding on their parts. At some point, the conversation had become very real.

And that's what made him nervous.

She had the right idea. They'd pretend it hadn't happened and concentrate on work.

"We need to make a list of places we can go where we might find the type of young man we're looking for," she said slowly. "Maybe like gyms, places like that."

"Since we're in Texas, aren't you going to look at cowboys? There must be a lot of ranches around here."

"Cowboys."

That was all Tess said. Just the one word, but the way she said it made it pretty damn clear to Blake she thought it was a good idea. What was it with women and cowboys? So what if they could chase down cows. He'd like to see them try to rope the Neat and Tidy Cleaner account. That hadn't been a walk in the park.

"Yeah, fine, cowboys," he muttered, enjoying this trip less and less. "After breakfast we'll ask the concierge about ranches and rodeos. There must be something nearby."

Before she could answer, a waitress appeared to take their order. Tess happily chatted with the other woman, acting as though she didn't have a care in the world. After the waitress finally left, Blake rubbed at the tightness in his neck. He'd be hard-pressed to think of an assignment he'd enjoyed less than this one. But landing Desire Perfume could be their ticket, so he'd put up with a lot to make that happen.

"Tell me more about your idea for this campaign," he said. "Let's assume we'll have luck and find the perfect candidate and that his background check turns out okay. What next?"

Tess finally made eye contact with him, and he felt a jolt of awareness zap through him. The sensation disconcerted him for a second. What was going on here? Tess really couldn't be getting to him...could she?

"I guess I covered most of it last night," she said. "We can show him as he is now, then treat him to some kind of a makeover with a new haircut, maybe put him in a tux. Then we'll do the after picture."

"You want to smooth off all the rough edges."

"A few of them, but certainly not all. That's what makes these young men different. They'll still be real people. And a real man is always more attractive to a woman than some pretty pinup picture."

"You sure about that?"

Tess gave him that determined look he'd come to expect from her over the last couple of days. "I'm absolutely positive about this."

As far as Blake was concerned, Jason had greatly underestimated his half sister when he'd said she wouldn't be of any help to them on the creative side of the business. Tess was sharp, and he liked her spin on this campaign. Only problem was making it work on such short notice.

He saw the waitress heading their way with breakfast. Soon, they'd find out exactly how much of a snowball's chance they had of finding a candidate today.

"Let's hope you find a cowboy quickly," he said. "Else those guys at the rodeo won't be the only ones trying their hardest not to step in a real mess."

TESS HAD never been on a ranch before, but it was pretty much what she'd expected. Lots of animals and noise and excitement. Thankfully, there were also lots of cowboys around. One of them had to be the man they needed for the campaign.

"See anyone interesting?" Blake asked.

"We just got here. Mind giving me a minute?"

He stood way too close to her for comfort, and Tess took a step forward wanting to put some much-needed space between them. The man made her nuts. All morning, they'd driven around checking various places the concierge had recommended. So far, they hadn't had much luck. But it was barely noon, so they still had time. That is, if she found someone quickly.

Idly rubbing her left temple, she surveyed the area. They were in the small town of Kinley, about forty miles outside of Dallas. Two weekends a month, the town held a rodeo. Thankfully, one was planned for this upcoming weekend, and even though it was only Thursday, many of the cowboys had already arrived and were practicing at a ranch on the outskirts of town.

"I don't know if any of these boys will be interested in modeling for you," said Jack Davison, the owner of the ranch. "But what the heck, I'll introduce you around."

Tess trailed after him, wondering if her plan would actually work. Maybe she should simply pick one of the models and be done with this. Debra would be happy. Blake would be happy. And she could go back to Chicago and forget all about this idea of hers. For all she knew, it wouldn't work. Maybe Debra would hate it. But since she and Blake had gone to so much trouble, she might at least look around the ranch.

"Are any of these young men charismatic?" Tess asked.

Jack stopped and turned to look at her, a wide grin

splitting his face. "Charismatic? Yeah, I guess a couple of them are 'cause women circle around them like flies around a big pile of..." His grin grew even larger. "Charisma."

Great. Just great. Tess was starting to think her idea was a pile of charisma as well.

"Why don't we start with those cowboys?" Blake said, moving up to stand next to Tess. "Tess here is a sucker for a guy full of charisma."

Jack snickered and headed off again. Tess refused to look at Blake. He was teasing her again, but Tess ignored him. In the last few days, she'd decided Blake was incapable of taking her seriously. It no longer annoyed her. In fact, it made things so much easier. If Blake continued to tease her, then she wouldn't act on this foolish attraction she felt for him.

They reached a corral where several young men stood around laughing and joking.

"Listen up, these two folks are from Chicago. An advertising agency," Jack hollered. "They want to talk to some of you boys, so be nice."

Still snickering, Jack walked away. Tess smoothed her hands down the sides of her slacks, wishing she'd worn jeans, like Blake had. But she hadn't packed any jeans, so navy linen slacks would have to do.

A couple of the young men were eyeing them with open curiosity, but most of them had turned their attention back to the man riding a horse inside the corral.

"See anybody interesting?" Blake asked again.

Tess studied a couple of cowboys who were staring

at them. One grinned, showing a gaping hole where several teeth should be.

"Stop asking me that," she told Blake, moving forward slowly. How exactly did a sophisticated woman approach a group of men and casually announce she wanted to turn one of them into a loverboy? At this moment, she longed to return to Chicago and spend her days in her office with her computer and adding machine. She wasn't good at this sort of thing, but truthfully, she had to wonder if anyone was good at this sort of thing.

Blake moved forward and walked next to her. A quick glance at him showed his grin was every bit as wide as Jack's had been. He loved this, seeing her get flustered and unnerved by a bunch of twenty-year-olds.

"See anyone interesting yet?" Blake asked once again without looking at her.

You. The thought hopped into her mind, and she immediately shoved it right back out.

Tess stopped and looked down at her sensible leather flats, so very out of place on this rustic ranch. She felt like those shoes, way out of her element, not only on this ranch, but also in her dealings with Blake. Even now, when she should have a witty retort, her heart was slamming against her ribs with a crazy rumba beat. Darn his handsome hide.

Drawing a deep, calming breath into her lungs, Tess studied the men around the corral and said, "When I see someone interesting, you will be the very first to..."

She froze. "Bingo."

"Which one? The guy on the horse?" Blake obviously knew she'd found the right man because his entire attitude had changed. He was all business now, the teasing gone from his voice.

Tess looked at the man riding the horse, shook her head, and turned her attention back to the young blond man standing off to one side of the corral. He was helping a boy of about twelve try to lasso a bale of hay and when the boy succeeded, he laughed and ruffled the youngster's hair.

"That one," she said, nodding in the direction of her candidate.

Blake chuckled. "You're a sentimentalist, Tess," he said, heading toward the blond man. "You picked the guy helping a kid."

Although he didn't say it, she knew that Blake meant she was sappy. But she didn't care. The fact that the best-looking young man also happened to be good with kids was just icing on the cake. She'd picked him because he was good-looking in a purely natural way.

As they walked over, she couldn't help wishing that the Loverboy candidate would drive her pulse crazy the way Blake did. But, unfortunately, no such luck. When they were close, the young man looked up, and even though intellectually Tess knew he was what the young women in the office called a babe, he didn't drive her hormones insane. Not like Blake.

"Can I help you folks?" the young man asked.

Blake introduced them, then turned to Tess and raised one eyebrow. Great, he'd left her with the difficult part to explain.

"I'm Tyler Roberts," the young man said. He draped his arm around the boy's shoulders. "This is my brother, Danny."

Tyler was too perfect. Tess quickly explained about the Loverboy cologne campaign and what they needed. As she spoke, the young man listened carefully. By the time her explanation was over, Tyler was already nodding.

For the first time since her half brother took off with no notice, Tess felt optimistic. Things were going to work out after all.

"Would the money be good?" Danny Roberts asked, nudging his brother.

Blake chuckled. "A businessman after my own heart. I take it you might be interested."

"Oh, yeah. I'm interested," Tyler said. "I could use the money. I'm buying a ranch, so where do I sign?"

He definitely was too perfect. Tess shot a smug look at Blake, who gave her a rueful smile. He knew they'd hit paydirt.

"It's not a guarantee, Tyler," Blake explained. "We need to shoot some preliminary pictures, find out about you—"

Wanting to get all the cards on the table, Tess said, "We'll have to run a background check on you. We can't invest all this money only to find out you've got some terrible secret in your past."

Tyler groaned. "Please tell me a traffic ticket won't be enough to stop you from hiring me. I didn't mean to get it, I was just listening to a CD, and I didn't notice—"

Blake held up one hand. "If that's the worst we find, it won't be a problem. But there are a lot of things we need to do before this becomes official. And you need to find out about us. Don't say yes until you've had time to make certain we're legitimate."

Blake was right, of course. Tess knew that. A lot of things had to happen before they even considered hiring this young man. But her feeling of optimism simply wouldn't go away. Handling the details might take some time and a lot of work, but she knew down to her toes in her oh-so-out-of-place flats that they'd found their first Loverboy model.

She smiled to herself, feeling very happy. Maybe she wasn't as bad at this as she'd thought.

BLAKE LEANED BACK against the bar and studied Tess. She was looking for him, and for a second, he simply watched her. Although tonight was supposed to be a celebratory dinner, she looked like she was going to a funeral. A very formal, business funeral. She had on one of her boxy suits and her hair was twisted back into that bun thing again.

Waving the young female bartender over, he asked, "Where's a fun place around here to eat?"

The woman flashed him a flirty smile. "Fun, how?"

Oh, yeah. He didn't have to be alone tonight if he didn't want to be. The lady made her point loud and clear. Too bad he wasn't interested in receiving the message. A few years ago, things would have been different. But just like he didn't get involved in long-term relationships, he also didn't do one-night stands.

Without intending to, he glanced toward Tess again. She'd spotted him and made her way between the small round tables scattered throughout the room. Tonight really was a celebration. Things looked as if they'd work out fine with Tyler, and Blake had to admit, Tess's instincts were dead-on. The kid was as handsome as any of the models they'd met, but he also came across as a real person, one concerned about his family, and terrific with his brother. He'd sell a million bottles of cologne.

So Blake had suggested this dinner to reward themselves. But Tess looked even more stiff and starched than usual. The lady didn't seem to have the word fun in her vocabulary.

"Fun as in entertaining," he said to the bartender, figuring dead men had a better chance of having a good time tonight than he did.

Tess had reached his side. The bartender studied her, then turning back to Blake said, "What you need is The Desperado Steakhouse. It's a Dallas favorite and should be right up your alley." With one more flirty, suggestive smile, she added, "But if things don't turn out the way you want, stop by again. I'm here until midnight."

She winked at Blake, then walked away to wait on another customer. When Blake turned his attention to Tess, she looked ready to spit bullets.

"I see you managed to amuse yourself while you waited," she said to him.

Blake laughed. "You're doing your schoolmarm thing again, Tess." Taking her arm, he added, "Come on, let's go try this steakhouse. I'm hungry, and you can be disapproving on the way over."

To his surprise, Tess closed her eyes and drew in a deep breath. He'd bet she was counting to ten. Or maybe twenty. Or more than likely, one hundred. But when she opened her eyes again, her gaze locked with his. For a nanosecond, Blake felt the blood in his veins hum. What was it about uptight Tess that got to him?

"You're right. I don't want to argue, especially not tonight," she said. "I'm very pleased with how things went today."

Her easy acquiescence startled Blake, but hey, he'd take a truce any day of the week. When they exited the hotel, they headed to their rental car, then drove to the steakhouse. He vowed to be on his best behavior tonight. The two of them had to continue working together for several more weeks. He needed to find a way for them to get along. Taking her to dinner would help them to relax and enjoy themselves.

Or not. As soon as they walked into the steakhouse, Blake knew this wasn't Tess's sort of place. Not her sort of place at all. The Desperado Steakhouse was loud, rowdy, and packed with people interested in serious fun.

Nope, not Tess's sort of place at all.

He thought about suggesting they leave, but the woman behind the hostess's desk laughed and shook her finger at Tess.

"Oh, no. Not here. We don't allow suits and ties in The Desperado Steakhouse." She nodded toward the chalkboard over her shoulder. Sure enough, written in large letters was the message: You're Here To Have A Good Time. Proper Attire Required. No Jackets. No Ties.

Tess gave Blake a befuddled look. "What kind of restaurant is this?"

"I guess one that takes fun seriously," he offered. "Want to go someplace else?"

The hostess laughed again and tugged on Blake's arm. "Don't go. You two look like you could use a nice night out on the town." She smiled at Tess. "Check your jacket and let your hair down. I bet you've worked hard all week. Have a little fun."

The look Tess gave him was reminiscent of a drowning man, but before Blake could do more than say "It's up to you," Tess had checked her coat and they were being led to a table facing the dance floor and stage.

"Just wait. You're going to have a hoot," the hostess assured them.

"I'm not sure I feel like having a hoot," Tess said, fidgeting with her white blouse. Rather than looking casual, she looked uncomfortable. She also looked pretty, her face lit from the soft candle burning in a small glass shaped like the state of Texas.

For a moment, he allowed himself to study her face—a determined chin, a small nose, and clear eyes that saw way too much. Why hadn't he noticed from the beginning what a pretty face Tess had?

More importantly, why the hell was he noticing now?

"So do you want to leave?" he asked more gruffly than he intended.

Tess shook her head. "No. We're here and I've checked my jacket. We might as well stay for dinner."

But after they'd placed their order and silence fell around them, Blake started to think that staying hadn't been such a good idea after all. This was about as much fun as a root canal.

"I think that kid Tyler is a good choice," he said.

Tess brightened immediately. "He does seem perfect, doesn't he? I have a good feeling about him."

"You were dead on the money with your idea," he said, taking a sip of his iced tea. "The models would make consumers think only perfect-looking people could wear Loverboy. Tyler should clean up nicely."

"I agree. He'll be great."

Some strange emotion made him tell her, "You're good at advertising, Tess. You seem to have a real feel for what will work."

Tess beamed at his compliment. "I only hope I'm right. Do you really think Debra will like this idea?"

"I'm certain of it. Especially after she sees Tyler."

She smiled at him, and he couldn't help smiling back. After a couple of seconds, the weirdest thing happened. The atmosphere around them slowly thickened with awareness. Sexual awareness. Before he knew what hit him, carnal images of his partner darted through his head. Heat flooded his body, and he found it impossible to look away from her.

A dull flush colored her cheeks. She felt the pull between them, too, and no doubt she wasn't any more pleased about it than he was.

Lust punched him in the gut, and the more he tried

to rein in his libido, the more it took off on dangerous treks into the realm of the erotic. What would Tess look like when aroused? Would she let down her guard and give herself over to passion? Would she use her considerable intellect to find new ways to please her partner? Would she—

The waitress appeared next to their table with their dinners, effectively dousing the steamy wanderings of Blake's brain.

Damn.

The conversation while they ate was nonexistent. Finally, desperate to break the tension, he asked, "Heard anything from Jason lately?"

Tess was toying with her tossed salad, but now she stopped and looked at him. "Not since the original phone message saying he wanted to go figure out his life."

Blake shook his head. "Man, I just don't understand this. Why would he take off like that? Where is he, and when is he coming back?"

Her sigh was heartfelt. "You have to stop worrying about him. The men in my family do this sort of thing all the time. My father's disappeared at least a dozen times."

This was news to him. "Are you serious? What about his family?"

"Family is no problem," she said, her voice overly bright. "If his wife doesn't understand, he gets a new wife. Jason's mom complained, so he married my mom. When my mom complained, he married wife number three."

"I'm sorry, Tess."

She shrugged. "Don't feel sorry for me. Feel sorry for current wife number five. It's only a matter of time until he disappears on her."

Blake had no idea what to say. In his book, her father was a selfish bastard.

"Jason has done this before," Tess told him. "Just once, right before college. That time, I assumed he'd only taken off to blow off some cobwebs before hitting the books. Now I worry that he'll turn out like Dad, disappearing at the drop of a hat." She looked at Blake. Her hazel eyes gazed steadily at him. "But what upsets me the most is he disappeared on you. His friend. This agency was Jason's idea. He had no right to drop it in our laps. It makes me..."

"Mad?" Blake supplied.

"Yes, mad." Indignation was visible in her eyes. "He shouldn't have done this to you. You're not part of our family. You're not used to this sort of behavior. As Jason's friend, you invested in this business, then he takes off like this? It's so unfair to you."

As much as Blake appreciated her outrage on his behalf, he needed to set a few things straight. "To us. It's unfair to us. None of this is your fault, Tess."

"Still, it's wrong, and I feel badly."

"Must have been difficult growing up around Jason and your dad."

When she looked at him this time, he could clearly see her aggravation and pain although she tried to mask it. Despite her tough exterior, Tess was a softie at heart.

"You never knew what they were going to do," she said, turning her attention back to her salad. "But Jason shouldn't have started D&S if he didn't intend on sticking around. You can't run a business if one of the partners takes off whenever the whim hits him."

Blake had to agree with her there. So far, he wasn't thrilled with the way Jason was acting. But he didn't want to say anything that would make Tess even more upset.

"It will work out," was all he could think to say. Without thinking, he reached across the small table and placed his hand over hers. She stiffened for a moment, but she made no effort to pull her hand away. Her skin felt so soft he almost pulled his hand away instead, but he didn't. Tess would misinterpret the move.

"You know, I think we're doing a fine job on our own," he said, meaning it. "Your idea about using real guys is better than anything Jason or I would have come up with."

Once again, a compliment of his made her beam. Blake got the annoying feeling that Tess hadn't received nearly enough compliments in her life. The smile she gave him was downright brilliant.

With a teasing laugh, she asked, "Are you feeling okay? That's the second time tonight you've said something nice to me."

"Cute."

A small band climbed the stairs to the stage across from them and started setting up their equipment.

"Looks like it's time for us to go," Tess said, slowly

removing her hand from his with more than a trace of self-consciousness.

Suddenly, he wasn't in a hurry to leave. He didn't want to go back to his hotel room and think about the phone conversation they'd shared the night before. He'd rather stay here.

"Let's listen to one or two songs before we go, okay?" he asked.

After a brief hesitation, Tess relented. "Okay. But after that, we need to head back. Our flight is at nine tomorrow, and I don't want to miss it."

As he'd expected, the band played country music. The first song was loud and wild, and even Tess seemed to be keeping time with the upbeat tempo. The second song was almost as fast, but the lyrics were about a man locked out of his house by his irate wife. The more the man tried to bargain with her, the madder his wife became. By the time the song ended, the entire audience was laughing.

Tess stood and looked at him. "This has been fun," she said loudly. "But I'd like to leave."

Blake stood and pushed in his chair, intending to follow her out of the restaurant. But the band launched into the sweet strains of a sad love song, and Tess stopped dead in her tracks. Leaning toward her, Blake put his mouth near her ear so she could hear him and asked, "Something wrong?"

"No. I just love this song."

He was so close, her floral perfume tantalized him. Without considering the wisdom of his actions, he took her hand and tugged her gently toward the dance floor.

"We should be going," Tess protested.

Blake simply shook his head and slid his arms around her waist. She didn't immediately move close, so he said, "I promise not to bite."

When she gave him one of her schoolmarm looks, he chuckled and added, "Unless, of course, you ask me nicely."

With an incredibly loud sigh that he knew she didn't mean, she slipped into his arms without further prompting. He wasn't certain why he'd asked her to dance, but now that he held her in his arms, he didn't care. She felt damn good there.

Pulling her a little bit closer, his heart beat faster when she placed one hand on his shoulder. She said something, but he couldn't hear her, so he moved closer still, dipping his head so her lips were near his ear.

"I'm not a good dancer," she said, her voice breathless and purely female.

He leaned back far enough to look at her face. Her eyes widened as he trailed one finger down the side of her cheek.

"You're doing fine," he said, not knowing if she could hear him or not. But he didn't care. Maybe it was because it had been a long time since he'd held a lady in his arms. Or maybe it was because Tess had let her prim and proper mask slip on this trip, showing him a peek at the woman underneath. But whatever the reason, he wanted to keep dancing with her, enjoying the feel of her body against his.

When he pulled her close this time, she melted against him, and he ran one hand down her back, settling it near her waist. Her breasts pressed against his chest, her legs slid against his. Desire twisted inside him, firing his blood. Lost in the sensation of her, he placed a soft kiss on the side of her neck.

"Blake, I don't think this is a good idea," she said, but she turned toward his kiss rather than away from it.

"Don't think so much," he said, trailing a trio of kisses around her jaw.

The band reached the final, haunting strains of the love song just as he lifted his head to look into Tess's eyes. The impulse that flooded him was stupid and dangerous. Really, *really* stupid.

His gaze dropped to her lips, which were parted slightly and looked oh-so-soft.

"Blake—" Her voice was that of a woman aroused.

Ignoring all the warning bells clanging in his head, Blake did the one thing he knew he shouldn't do.

He leaned down and kissed Tess. Hard.

4

THE LAST THING Tess expected was for Blake to kiss her, but when he did, she felt a jolt of desire zing through her body. Without hesitation, she kissed him back. Deeply, completely. Blake was a world-champion, take-home-the-blue-ribbon kisser, and when he ran the tip of his tongue over her bottom lip, she didn't hesitate to part her lips.

Heaven. Kissing him was heaven. She slid her arms around his neck and turned herself over to the fantasy. She never thought Blake would kiss her, but now that he was, she intended on enjoying every single second. In fact, she was so caught up in the feel and taste of Blake Sutherland that she forgot all about their surroundings until a harried waitress edging past the dance floor bumped into her.

Tess pulled away from Blake, breaking the contact reluctantly.

"Ooops, sorry," the waitress said to Tess and Blake as she moved passed them. "Didn't mean to bust things up."

Tess nodded absently, her attention focused completely on Blake. He looked as stunned by what had happened as she felt.

With a blink, Blake recovered first. He flashed a half

smile at the middle-aged waitress. "No problem. We should have picked a better place to do that."

The waitress winked at Tess. "Sometimes you gotta do it when the urge grabs you."

Tess smiled weakly as reality slammed into her. Blake had kissed her. Really kissed her. And she'd kissed him back.

No, no, no. This wasn't good. Not at all.

Tess was debating how to handle the situation when Blake placed his hand on her arm. "Let's head back to the hotel."

That stopped her dead in her tracks. She gave him a suspicious look. "What exactly do you mean by that? Because if you think one kiss—"

Blake chuckled and held up his hand. "Whoa. I wasn't suggesting we scramble back to the hotel so I can have my wicked way with you."

Great. Now she felt like an idiot. She took a deep breath and tried again. "Of course you weren't. I didn't think you were."

A smile still teased at his lips, but he didn't say a word. He merely waited for her to precede him toward the exit of the restaurant. But as she went to walk by him, he leaned down and said, "Unless you want to. I'm easy."

She tipped her head and looked at him. This close, she could smell the faint scent of sandalwood, no doubt from the soap he used. The smell teased at her senses, trying to seduce her, but she ignored it. "I'm not."

"Yeah, I've noticed that. But don't worry, we'll keep working on it."

His response seemed so serious, so sincere, that Tess couldn't help but laugh, earning her a grin from Blake.

"You're insane," she said, walking by him and heading for the door. "Completely, certifiably insane."

And so was she. Without a single protest, she'd kissed Blake back. Didn't she know how dumb that was? Blake Sutherland could be the posterboy for charming guys. He had the routine down pat. The smile. The teasing manner. Sure, they'd had a nice evening. But that was no excuse. She should have stopped him before he'd kissed her. Barring that, she should have stopped him the second his lips had touched hers.

Instead she'd melted like butter in the hot sun.

After retrieving her jacket, they left. Halfway across the parking lot, Tess faced facts. Kissing Blake was a huge mistake, but understandable. He was, after all, incredibly sexy. But she'd indulged her little fantasy, so now she simply needed to make certain nothing like this ever happened again.

"I read in *American Scientist* that your brain can literally explode if you think too hard," Blake said when he got even with her. "Happens all the time."

"Ha. Ha. Guess that's something you don't have to worry about."

Blake chuckled as he unlocked the rented sedan and opened the passenger-side door for her. "You know, Tess, I really like you."

His comment was unexpected. For a second, she

looked at him, wondering if he was sincere. She shouldn't care if he liked her, but oddly, she did.

"You're not all that bad either," she said as she slid inside the car.

Blake's laugh was loud and long. "Thanks for puffing up my ego."

On the drive back to the hotel, he picked up the conversation again. "No, I'm serious. Thinking too hard isn't good for you."

"My brain isn't about to explode," she maintained, although she wasn't one hundred percent certain that was true. The pain in her right temple was taking on monumental proportions.

"But you are fussing over what happened. It was just a kiss, Tess. Maybe I shouldn't have done it, but hey, it's not like I kicked you in the kneecaps. No harm. No foul. It didn't mean anything."

She was glad he felt that way. But to make absolutely certain, she wanted to make a few things crystal clear to him right now to avoid possible confusion. "That's right. The kiss didn't mean anything. More importantly, we can never do that again. We have a business to run."

Blake ran one hand through his hair. "The kiss was an impulse, Tess. A dumb impulse, I'll grant you. But only an impulse. Still, if it will make you feel better, when we get back to Chicago, we'll rent a boat and take a sail on Lake Michigan. Once we get far away from land, you can keelhaul me a couple of times. Sound fair?"

For the second time in the past few minutes, he made

her laugh. She didn't feel like laughing, not at all, but a laugh slipped out of her mouth. The man was a menace. "Sounds fair."

"And since the kiss obviously upset you, I promise to keep my lips to myself in the future." He pulled into the hotel parking lot and found a spot. "How about you?"

"How about me what?" After he turned off the car, she unfastened her seatbelt, anxious to escape. Anxious to get away from him. She shoved open her door, then glanced at him. His face was clearly visible in the bright overhead light.

Blake placed a hand on her arm, preventing her exit. "Do *you* plan on keeping *your* lips to yourself?"

"You don't have to worry about *my* lips." She shoved her door open a little wider and made a move to get out, but again, Blake stopped her.

"You sure? Because I know you'd like to think the kiss is all my fault, but you did participate."

The gleam in his eyes made it clear he wanted her to lighten up. She knew he was right. They needed to agree the kiss was an impulse that would never, ever happen again and then forget about it.

But deep in her soul, she knew forgetting about Blake's kiss would be difficult. For her, at least. She'd never experienced a kiss that made her feel so alive. So sensual and sexy.

But she had to be practical about this.

"You don't have to worry, Blake. I won't kiss you," she assured him.

He grinned, that bad-boy grin of his that made her IQ drop. "Promise?"

"*Yes.* I promise."

He removed his hand from her arm and opened his own door. "Great, because I'd hate to spend the next few weeks worrying about my virtue."

Does this guy ever stop? Tess climbed out of the car. Although she would have preferred talking about the kiss without all the jokes, she was glad they'd flattened this issue. They'd kissed. It had been good, more than good, at least for her. But it would never happen again. She and Blake had far too many things to worry about without mixing attraction into the equation. They needed to keep their minds on Loverboy.

As far as she could tell, the only tiny flaw in her plan was that now she knew Blake's kisses were hot enough to melt a polar icecap.

TODAY'S MEETING with Debra Tomlin was a damn sight different than the last one. For starters, this time she wasn't flirting with him. Not in the least. In fact, for the most part, she ignored him.

Worked for him. Since these ads were Tess's brainchild, she should be the one to present the concept anyway. At the moment, Tess was explaining her idea using a mock-up of what she envisioned for the print ads. She'd used one of the casual pictures they'd taken of Tyler standing next to his brother. Tess explained that his before picture would look something like this, with Tyler in his rodeo clothes.

"A cowboy," Debra raised one brow and looked at

Blake. "Is he a real cowboy or just some guy who likes to dress up?"

"Real. Tess and I hung around at the rodeo practice for a while. The kid's pretty good at roping cows."

Debra chuckled and turned to Tess. "A cowboy, huh? Clichéd, but effective. This kid will work, but make certain we don't end up with a line-up that looks like a group of male strippers."

"We won't," Tess hurriedly assured her, and Blake didn't miss the pink color that faintly tinted Tess's cheeks. "In fact, on the print ads, we plan to identify Tyler as a rodeo competitor, not as a cowboy."

"Should work." Debra shoved back her chair and stood, so Blake stood as well. She looked at Tess. "Use the brother in the ad, too. He's cute."

Then with that, she headed toward the door, saying over her shoulder as she walked, "Work out the details and get the first ad out there."

Blake sprinted over and opened the conference room door for Debra just in time for her to breeze through. He was all set to walk her out when he noticed Tess hanging back. He frowned at her, then when she made it clear she intended on letting him walk Debra out by himself, he waved her over.

"I'm very happy with how this campaign is shaping up," Debra told him as they headed toward the front exit.

"Thanks. The idea was Tess's." Blake wanted to make certain Debra knew who deserved the credit.

"It doesn't really matter who thought of it," Tess

said as she fell in step with them. "We work as a team here at D&S."

Blake stopped, blocking enough of the hallway that Debra stopped as well. He looked at the older woman. "We are a team, but I feel it's important you know who thought of using regular guys."

When he glanced briefly at Tess, he could clearly read surprise on her face, which annoyed him. Did she think he would steal her idea? Too many times when he'd worked for Markland and Jacobs, his ideas were credited to others. No way would he let that happen at his own agency.

Debra smiled and patted Tess on the arm. "Good for you. I like the idea. But you need to take after Blake here. Don't be shy. Tell the world what you've done. Women tend to be too nice in business sometimes." With a laugh she added, "Not me, of course. But some women."

Then, arching one brow, she asked Blake, "Anything else?"

He shook his head and escorted her the rest of the way out. After Debra was gone, Blake looked at Tess.

"Deb sort of reminds me of a tornado," he said.

"Absolutely." As they walked past Molly's desk, Tess added, "By the way, you didn't need to make such an issue about who thought of the idea."

"*Yes*, I did." Noticing that Molly was listening to their every word, Blake nodded toward his office. "Let's talk."

Tess hesitated. And he knew why. That damn kiss again. Did she think he was going to toss her on the desk and try to get her out of her button-down suit? For starters, he didn't have time right now to tackle such an imposing task. The lady was trussed up tighter than those cows they'd seen at the ranch.

Beyond that, he was fairly certain fooling around with Tess in his office violated their agreement. Sure, the exact agreement had been no more kissing. But Tess probably had meant to include desk sex on her list of no-nos, too.

"What are you grinning about?" she asked.

He was grinning? He hadn't meant to be. "Nothing."

She narrowed her eyes. "You know, just when I think you're a nice guy by making certain Debra knows the idea was mine, you blow it. You've got a wicked grin on your face. I don't even want to know what you're thinking about."

With a chuckle, he looped his arm through hers and tugged her toward his office. "I'm not thinking anything. Come on. Let's talk."

"We should go back to the conference room and help finalize the plans with Annie and Drew."

Blake tugged her arm again. "They know what to do. You and I need to talk."

When she still hesitated, Blake sighed. "It was one little kiss, Tess. You can't avoid me forever because of one kiss."

She started shushing him long before he'd said his peace, but he ignored her. He wasn't the one refusing to discuss this in his office. He didn't want to talk about their working relationship in the lobby with Molly listening, but hey, it was her decision.

Tess gave him another of her schoolmarm looks and headed to his office, muttering about him as she went. As crazy as it sounded, he kind of liked the way she looked when she had had enough. Her face became flushed; her eyes sparkled. Angry was a good look for her.

Of course, he'd never tell her that. She'd stomp him flatter than a bug.

"*What* are you grinning at now?" she demanded again once she'd reached the privacy of his office.

Damn. He'd been grinning again? The only excuse he had was the relief he felt that Tess was finally talking *to* him, not over his left shoulder. Ever since the kiss last week, she'd avoided having a direct conversation with him. It felt good to finally have her look him in the eye.

"You're acting goofy today," she said, dropping into one of the chairs facing his desk.

Rather than sit behind his desk, he chose to lean against the front of it. That put him precariously close to her, but he wanted her complete attention. However when her light flowery scent filled his lungs, he questioned his own wisdom at getting so near to her.

What was it about Tess in her button-down suit that made him want to stand up and howl? She wasn't his type. Not even remotely. Maybe that was it. Maybe his reaction to her was a case of the appeal of the unknown.

For starters, who knew what she hid under her boxy

suits? While they'd been dancing he'd felt curves on her, but they were well cloaked. And then there was her mind. He didn't understand how Tess's mind worked. For the most part, she was so structured, always in control. Probably because the men in her family were so out of control.

But every once in a while, mostly when she was aggravated at him, he saw fire in Tess. The same fire he'd felt in her kiss.

That damnable fire kept praying on his mind. Kissing her had been hot. And now he found himself thinking way too much about her. Wondering about things he had no business wondering about.

Tess's annoyed voice sliced right through his musing. "What is with you today? You've got this weird look on your face."

"Sorry," he muttered. Business. He needed to focus on business. What had they been talking about? Oh yeah. Debra. "Now that we've got the go-ahead, we need to set up the shoot with Tyler, then move on to the next city. I thought Madison would be good," he said.

"Sounds fine. I'll do some preliminary work this week while you and Annie handle Tyler's shoot."

Blake nodded, and deciding to be smart for a change, moved over to his side of the desk and sat. "So we'll leave for Madison next Monday. I'll have Molly make the arrangements. We'd both better figure that for the next couple of months, we'll be out of town every other week."

Tess frowned. "About that, maybe it would be better if you took Annie or Drew with you on these trips."

Her comment didn't surprise him. He'd been expecting her to try to back out. "We went over this before we headed to Dallas. I want *you* to pick the men we use in the campaign." Leaning forward, he asked, "Is this your way of saying you'd rather I didn't go with you?"

"No," she said, although she wasn't making eye contact with him again and the sigh she treated him to was loud and dramatic. "You need to be equally involved."

"Ah, hell. Is this about the kiss? Stop worrying. I'm not going to kiss you again." His gaze never left her face while he waited for her to finally look at him. When she did, he said, "Tess, we need to be adults about this and move on. It's been four days. Have my lips come anywhere near you?"

Tess sat up even straighter in her chair. Great. Now she was in extreme schoolmarm mode. He braced himself.

"No. You've been fine," she told him. "But I don't know how wise it is for us to work so closely together. Especially when we're out of town."

"Hey, my lips are trustworthy. So if you still have doubts, it must be because you don't trust yourself."

Wow. If looks could kill, the one she was giving him right now would have him drawn and quartered. This he could deal with. Tess running at full alert he could handle. At least she wasn't worrying about the kiss anymore.

He bit back a smile and said, "Never mind."

Tess's eyes were definitely silver now. "I'm not going to have an affair with you."

She couldn't have surprised him more if she'd hit

him with a fish. "What? What gave you the idea I wanted us to have an affair? No offense, but having an affair would really mess up everything."

Talk about an understatement. They needed the Loverboy campaign to be a hit so they could get the money they needed. Neither one of them could afford to get distracted right now.

An affair? Hell, they couldn't seem to get beyond a kiss.

He ran his hands through his hair, trying to get a handle on this situation.

"Tess, you really think that not traveling together will prevent us from having an affair? What's your plan then? You go with Annie? Or would you rather go with Drew? No, wait, that won't work because Drew is young and attractive, and you might end up having an affair with him instead."

Tess's look was downright glacial. "Cute. Real cute, Blake. It's nice to know you're taking this seriously."

"I'm not taking it seriously because it doesn't deserve to be taken seriously. It was one stupid kiss."

Damn. He hadn't meant to sound so upset. But that's how he felt. What would the employees think if suddenly Tess refused to travel with him? Why was she being so difficult about this?

Blake gave her a half smile and tried again. "It was only one little kiss, Tess. Not the end of the world. I promise it won't happen again. Things will be fine in Madison."

Either his assurance helped, or he'd worn her down, because after a minute, she relented. "Fine. We'll try it again." Standing, she added, "I just don't want our relationship to become complicated."

He knew how she felt, and she was right. Neither of them wanted or needed this situation to become complicated. He'd do his part, and from the stubborn expression on her face, she'd do hers, too.

"It won't become complicated," he told her, but even as he said the words, he could only hope he was right. Deep in his soul, he wasn't so sure.

"I DON'T really know about modeling." The young man shifted his weight from one hip to the other. "I'm pretty busy with college and work."

Tess understood his reluctance. He must think they were insane, but she knew Alex Dumas was perfect for Loverboy. Absolutely perfect. The young man was not only attending medical school, he worked part-time, and he pitched in at a local food bank. In her book, that made him perfect Loverboy material.

"We won't take much of your time, and we can do the photo shoot here," Tess said, trying again to convince him. She glanced at Blake, who merely shrugged. "I'm sure you could use the money. College is expensive."

Alex's face reflected his indecision, and Tess held her breath. *Say yes*, she mentally chanted. She and Blake had spent two days searching Madison to find the right man. She'd finally gotten a brainstorm this morning and stopped off at the food bank. Alex had been working there, and she'd known immediately he was their second Loverboy.

The problem was Alex didn't want to be a Loverboy. She hadn't really planned on having a lot of resistance since Tyler had been anxious to sign up.

"Don't get me wrong, Ms. Denison. I could use the money. But I'm not the model sort."

"We're not going to take up more than an afternoon of your time," she explained, wishing she understood what the problem was. She looked again at Blake, who was focused on Alex.

"Would it help if we showed you the first ad in the series?" Blake offered.

Alex brightened at that. "Yes. I'd like to see it."

Tess got a folder out of her oversized purse. "We shot this last week. The young man is from Texas. He's saving up to buy a ranch."

Alex studied the ad closely, his expression unreadable. Tess knew if the ad itself didn't convince him, nothing would. On the left side, Tyler was shown in jeans and a plaid shirt. On the right was a picture of him and his brother, decked out in tuxedoes. The copy read: A True Loverboy Cares About His Family.

"Wow. This looks great. I thought you meant something that was...well, you know, racy," Alex said.

Bingo. Tess looked at Blake who gave her a half smile. Turning back to Alex, she said, "Your ad would be along the same lines. A shot on the left of you in your everyday clothes, and one on the right of you in a tuxedo."

Alex studied the photo in his hand again. "What will it say?"

"I don't know. Maybe a true Loverboy cares about

other people?" Tess suggested. When Blake made a face, she added, "Or something like that. We want to point out that the ideal man isn't about looks, it's about character. The type of man any woman would fall for. Someone who's making a difference in this world. That's what makes a man attractive, when he's got a soul."

Alex had his attention fully focused on Tess. "You think I'm like that?" He shook his head. "I'm not. I'm no one special."

Just the fact that he didn't think he was special made him special. Alex wasn't the sort to spend time primping in front of a mirror. He was out there making the world a better place.

Perfect for Loverboy.

"Yes, you're very special. And we want to convey that message. Sure, you'll look handsome in the ads. We do want to sell cologne. But I promise the ads will be very tasteful," she said, looking at Blake for confirmation. Blake, however, was frowning at her. He looked uncomfortable, which was odd. Well, she didn't have time to worry about Blake right now. Alex was wavering.

"Alex, we're not trying to make you look like some sort of player. You're a good-looking young man, but what makes you so attractive is that you help other people. You work at this food bank, you're studying to be a pediatrician. You're a great guy, and we want to show that."

When she finished speaking, she glanced again at

Blake, who finally got her silent message and joined in the conversation.

"Tess is right. You're a good kid. The kind who deserves credit for what he does." Blake patted Alex on the shoulder. "We don't want you to do anything that makes you uncomfortable. These ads will be great. Even your mom will think so."

Blake had obviously hit the right note. Alex grinned. "My mother will go crazy. She'll have a field day showing all her friends."

"Yeah, moms are that way," Blake said with a laugh. "Mine still drags out pictures from my kindergarten graduation. So what do you say? If all the legal stuff checks out, you want to do this?"

When Alex nodded, Tess breathed a silent sigh of relief.

"Sure," he said. "I can really use the money."

Tess felt like doing a victory dance. They'd landed Loverboy number two. After handling the details and making arrangements to get back in touch with Alex, Tess and Blake left the food bank.

"I am so jazzed," she said, once they were inside the rental car and heading back to the hotel. "Alex will be perfect in the ads."

Blake glanced at her briefly, but since he had on sunglasses, she couldn't see his eyes. He was oddly silent. A bad feeling settled in Tess's stomach.

"What? What's wrong? I thought Alex would make a good Loverboy model."

"He will," Blake said.

Well, at least his voice sounded normal, even pleasant. He wasn't angry, thank goodness.

"So, if you agree Alex is a great candidate, what's wrong?"

"Nothing."

Like she believed that. Whether she wanted to be or not, she'd become somewhat attuned to this man. At the moment, she could sense something was bothering him.

"You need to tell me what the problem is. If you think picking Alex was the wrong choice, I wish you had told me before I'd spent all that time convincing him to do it."

"I don't think he's wrong. I think he's completely right. And I think Debra will like the new slant you're taking. By focusing on more than just the young men's looks, you're sending a nice, subtle message."

She was? "I am?"

"Sure. Tyler takes care of his younger brother. Alex works in a food bank. They're good guys who, like you said, help other people."

"But I'm not trying to send a message, except that any man can be a Loverboy."

"You find men attractive who are the volunteer sort, the kind who pitch in and help out. The kind you can depend on."

Tess started to argue with him, but didn't. He was right. Both Tyler and Alex were dependable, helpful young men.

"Guess any first-year psych major can figure out

why I like dependable men," she said with a wry laugh. "I'm pretty transparent."

"No. You've got your priorities straight, and you like men who have theirs straight as well. The extra depth will help the Loverboy campaign."

"I'm glad you like it. So, if that's not the problem, what is?"

Blake glanced at her briefly, then looked back at the road. "What makes you think there's a problem?"

Tess fumbled around her neck. "Wait. Did I forget to wear my 'I'm not stupid necklace' today?"

With a soft chuckle, Blake said, "Boy, you don't give up, do you?"

There was a fairly good chance he didn't mean that as a compliment, but Tess took it as one anyway. "That's right. I'm persistent."

"That's one word for it."

When Blake stopped for a light, Tess leaned over and placed her hand on his arm. As always when she touched him, she felt a tingle dance across her skin.

"What's really bothering you?" she asked softly.

"Nothing is bothering me, Tess. I think Alex is great and will be a real asset to the campaign."

"But?"

He flashed her a quick smile before he returned his attention to the road. "Let's just hope there's an endless supply of good-looking saints."

"Oh, please. They don't have to be saints."

Blake swung the car into the hotel parking lot. After he parked, he tossed his sunglasses on the dash and looked at her. "Whatever. Let's just hope the world contains four more really hot guys who are out saving the world."

With that parting shot, he shoved open his car door and headed toward the entrance of the hotel. Tess sat in the car watching him walk away. What had just happened here? If she didn't know better, she'd think Blake was jealous.

That was ridiculous. Blake wasn't jealous. For starters, he'd made it more than clear that not kissing her again wasn't a hardship. On top of that, he had nothing to worry about when it came to looks. Blake Sutherland was hot—sizzling hot. He could melt ice in zero-degree weather.

"Yeah, sure, he's jealous," Tess muttered, climbing out of the car and locking the doors. "And I'm the Tooth Fairy."

5

BLAKE SAT in his mother's living room, thumbing through the stack of bills she'd given him. There were quite a few, but he could cover them. This time. Still, if the agency didn't take off soon, he'd have to consider getting another job if he was going to continue covering his expenses along with his mother's and his sister's.

And he would cover the bills. He owed his mother this. Kathleen Sutherland had worked day and night to take care of Blake and his sister, Lisa, after their father died. She was one tough lady. Even now, suffering with arthritis, his mother kept going. Kathleen was the first to pitch in at church, the one all her friends turned to for help.

He'd learned so many things from her when he was growing up—the value of hard work, the importance of family, and how to get up when you're knocked down. But mostly, he'd learned to go after his dreams. Kathleen was a big believer in pursuing dreams.

As soon as he possibly could, he'd pitched in around the house, trying to make dreams come true for all of them. At thirteen, he'd earned money running errands for the neighbors. At fourteen, he'd mowed lawns. By sixteen, he'd been working a job after school at the local movie theater. He'd gone through college on a scholarship, taking as many courses as possible, still working part-time. Only in the last few years had he finally felt like he had enough money to make life a little easier for all of them.

Of course, paying the bills had been easier when he'd worked for Markland and Jacobs. His salary at the big agency had been a lot more than what he and Tess could afford to take home now. But in the long run, leaner days now meant better days later if he and Tess could get the agency up and running.

"Sorry about those bills," his mother said, settling into the recliner across from him. "Everything costs so much and Social Security only goes so far."

"It's no problem," he assured her, tucking the bills into his jacket pocket. "I can cover them."

"I'm sure I could pick up some cleaning work if I asked the neighbors."

Blake shook his head, adamant about this point. "No. I can cover these bills, Mom. The agency is doing fine."

Kathleen folded her hands across her lap and fixed him with a purely maternal stare. "Are you telling me the truth, young man?"

Blake chuckled at her obvious attempt to make him feel like a four-year-old. "Have I ever lied to you?"

This time, she was the one to chuckle. "You don't really want me to answer that, do you?"

"Guess not." He settled back on the couch and studied her face. She looked good. Relaxed. Happy. He'd like to think that by easing her financial problems, he'd helped make her life more enjoyable. Once the agency was running at a profit and his sister was through grad school, he'd be able to set up an investment plan for his mother so she'd have a nest egg for the future. In the meantime, he'd keep covering her bills.

"Have you talked to Lisa lately?" he asked.

Kathleen rolled her eyes. "She's as bad as you are. Lisa's taking too many classes this semester, but there's no changing her mind. She's in a hurry to get out and make big bucks."

"Does she need anything?"

"You mean money. Yes, she could use some money." For a moment, she simply looked at him, her expression one of pride. "How did I ever get a son like you?"

"I don't know. Stood in the wrong place at the wrong time?"

Kathleen laughed. "Hardly." She got out of her chair, crossed the room, and placed a loud smacking kiss on his forehead. "You're the best son a mom could have," she said as she patted his cheek.

"Thanks. Let me take a sec and polish my halo."

His mother resettled in her recliner. "Seriously, you're a good man. Good enough that I'm only going to mention one time tonight that you should find a special woman and get married."

"I appreciate you only mentioning it once," Blake said, before he segued back to their original conversation. "I'll put some money in Lisa's account in the morning."

"She said she could get a job, that way you wouldn't

have to always be sending her money. I think it's a good idea."

"No." Blake was adamant about this. He'd promised his sister he'd put her through college, and he'd keep his promise. "Lisa can't focus on her classes if she's worrying about money. I've got it handled, Mom."

His mother gave him a soft, sweet look that tugged on Blake's heart. "I worry about you, honey. You take on so much responsibility. I know it's getting to you. You look tired."

Her comment caught him by surprise. "I'm not tired."

Kathleen made a tsking noise. "Yes, you are. You look like you've missed a lot of sleep putting in long hours at your agency."

He might look tired, but it wasn't because he'd been putting in long hours. It was because he'd been spending too much time thinking about Tess.

"I've been traveling," he told his mother, not wanting to share the real problem with her. "First Dallas. Then Madison. We leave for Charleston in a couple of days."

"It's not that." His mother narrowed her eyes, studying him closely. "Something is bothering you. I can tell."

Blake groaned. "The only thing bothering me is that you're playing mind reader. I'm fine, Mom."

His mother wasn't a woman who missed much. As a kid, Blake hadn't been able to get away with anything because his mom could always tell.

"I'm fine. Really," he reiterated. "So, tell me about the new hymn books at church."

Her narrow-eyed look grew even narrower. "Nice try, kiddo, but you're not shaking me off so easily. You might as well tell me what's on your mind. I'll find out sooner or later."

Blake hung his head. How many times had he heard her say the same words when he'd been growing up? At least a thousand.

And she was right. Sooner or later, she'd always figured out what was going on.

But not this time. She'd never guess he had the hots for his business partner and it was making it difficult to concentrate at work.

"So, you're not having any problems with Tess?" she asked.

"Nope, no problems," he told his mother, which was a complete lie. His attraction to Tess was driving him nuts. At least a half-dozen times a day, he found himself thinking about her. But he would find a way around this problem. Somehow.

Kathleen nodded, but Blake didn't buy for a second that she believed him. "I see. And that boy you found in Texas, what's his name?"

"Tyler Roberts."

"Right. Is he going to work out for you?" Her blue eyes, so like his own, studied him closely.

"Yes. So is the kid from Madison, Alex Dumas. The campaign looks great." He flashed his best grin. "Look ma, no problems."

"Okay, we'll play this your way. Don't tell me

what's going on. I'll figure it out," she said with a too-sweet smile on her face. "Let's see, what do I know?"

"Come on, Mom," Blake said with a laugh, but she ignored him and continued her Agatha Christie routine.

"You were fine before the trip to Dallas, but you've been distracted since you got back. I'll assume something happened while you were there." She templed her hands and looked at the ceiling. "You and Tess were on the trip by yourselves. Did you have a big fight?"

"No. You're wasting your time. There is no problem."

She ignored his protest. "Did you hear from Jason yet?"

Blake sighed with the knowledge that this exaggerated version of twenty questions could go on all night. "Jason being gone isn't a problem. It's nothing for you to worry about. But to answer your question, no we haven't heard from him. As far as I can tell, the guy has completely bailed on us. But Tess and I are doing fine on our own."

Surprisingly, that was true. A few weeks ago, he would have thought it impossible. But they did work well together. Now all he needed to do was find a way to dull the sizzling attraction between them.

So far, nothing he'd tried had worked, and the trip to Madison had only made the attraction between them stronger. He was way too aware of Tess. Hell, he'd even found himself getting upset when Tess had practically fawned over Alex. Sure, Alex was a great kid.

Handsome, a community volunteer. What wasn't there to like?

But Blake had felt a wave of jealousy wash over him while Tess talked to Alex. Him? Jealous of a twenty-one-year-old kid? He didn't think so.

What he needed was a no-fail way to douse the attraction between them. He kept thinking it would go away, or at the very least fade a little. But no such luck.

He spent way too much time fantasizing about a woman who knotted her hair up in a tight bun and wore clothes a nun would consider conservative. But that's what he kept doing, fantasizing about her. And he'd had some spectacular fantasies.

"You're certain you and Tess are getting along?"

Blake blinked and returned his attention to his mother. "Yeah. We're great."

"That's good," his mother said sweetly, although her expression was openly suspicious. "I'd like to meet Tess. She reminds me of you. Always doing the right thing."

Blake stared at his mother. She had to be kidding. "You're dead wrong. Tess is nothing like me. She's rigid and stuffy and…"

One hell of a kisser.

Blake forced the thought away. "Let's just say she's completely different."

His mother gave him a little half smile. "Really? Oh well, it's the differences that make life interesting."

Whoa. He didn't like the way his mother was looking at him. He needed to stop her before she got some crazy idea in her head. "Don't go there, Mom."

His mother smiled sweetly. "All I'm saying is that I'm sure you and Tess will be wonderful together."

Blake frowned. "Tess and I are business partners, that's all."

Kathleen's look was one of pure innocence, but again Blake didn't buy it for a minute. "Of course, dear, what else?"

"THESE SHOTS of Alex are hot," Annie said, walking into Tess's office the next morning. "The guy looks great. Every bit as good as Tyler."

Tess pulled her attention away from her computer and took the photographs from Annie. The younger woman was right. Alex looked great. He'd sell a lot of cologne. What woman wouldn't fall for a guy like him?

"He does look handsome." A few of the photos were of Alex in a T-shirt and jeans. The rest were of him in a tuxedo. Alex was very photogenic.

"He makes my heart go pitter-pat," Annie said with a laugh.

Tess only wished her heart went pitter-pat around Alex—or any other guy—the way it did every time Blake came near her. All her partner had to do was say hi, and she felt like her body had caught on fire.

It was incredibly depressing.

Tess set the photos down and looked at Annie. Tall and slim with shoulder-length black hair, she was pretty, friendly and smart.

"These shots are going to work fine," Tess told the younger woman. "Anything else?"

Annie dropped into the chair facing Tess's desk.

"Forgive me for asking, but are you okay? You seem distracted these days."

Tess liked Annie, she really did. They'd hit it off from the very beginning. But Tess couldn't talk to Annie about what was really bothering her. It wouldn't be appropriate.

So she settled for a lie. "I'm fine."

"Ah, yes. Fine." Annie slowly nodded her head. "A lot of people in this office are fine. Just yesterday, Blake told Drew he was fine."

Tess frowned. "I didn't know there was anything wrong with Blake."

Annie shrugged. "He says he's fine, but he seems distracted. Just like you do. And the rest of us have noticed you two seem to avoid each other when you're at the office."

The employees had noticed she was avoiding Blake? This wasn't good.

"We're not avoiding each other. We have a lot of work to do. With all these trips, we have so little time to catch up on things when we're in the office."

Annie sat forward in her chair, her expression somber. "It's just that Molly, Drew and I can't help wondering if everything's okay with the business. Jason's gone now, and I know we need this Loverboy account to succeed. Is the company having problems? Is that why you and Blake are so tense?"

Wow. This was the last thing Tess had expected. She hurried to reassure her co-worker. "Everything's fine with the business. Great, in fact. Two other companies called this week, wanting to meet with us about possible ad campaigns. D&S will have plenty of other work."

Annie looked relieved. "That's good."

"But you should know that once we finish Loverboy, Blake's going to buy me out. Advertising isn't really my line of work, but I'm sure the rest of you can stay on."

Tess had expected Annie to be upset, but instead, the younger woman simply nodded. "I know the ad business isn't your field, so I don't blame you for wanting to get out. Um, so you really think Blake will keep the rest of us on?"

"Absolutely," she said, glad to hear Annie wanted to stay. Blake would have enough problems without having to find new staff.

Annie stood, looking much more relaxed. "I'll tell the troops. Thanks, Tess, for letting us know what's happening." She took a couple of steps toward the door, then turned. "You know, when I first met Blake, I thought he'd be just like Jason. Handsome. Charming. Impossible to depend on. But he's not like that at all. He's actually very responsible. I like working for him. He's a nice boss."

With that, Annie left Tess's office. Tess tried turning her attention back to her work, but she couldn't. She kept thinking about what Annie had said. Blake really was a great boss. He went out of his way to make certain all of the employees felt at home and appreciated.

But Annie had also brought up a point Tess couldn't ignore. She and Blake couldn't keep avoiding each other. For the time remaining in this partnership, they needed to have a smooth working relationship. For goodness sake, they were both adults. They could put aside this annoying attraction and get the job done.

With a sigh, Tess stood and headed down the hall to Blake's office. She wasn't looking forward to this conversation. But now was not the time to have the employees distracted. Everyone needed to be focused on the Loverboy campaign.

Blake's office door was open, as always. Tess tapped lightly on the doorframe, and he looked up immediately.

"Got a second?" she asked, walking slowly into his office. She closed the door behind her. They needed to discuss the situation between them without the entire office overhearing.

Blake looked beyond Tess to the closed door before his deep blue gaze returned to her face. "Sure."

Tess took a couple of steps closer to his desk, uncertain how to begin this conversation. "You've been working a lot of hours since we got back from Madison."

"So have you." He nodded at the closed door. "What's up?"

She moved closer to his desk. "Annie stopped by my office a couple of minutes ago. She and the other employees have noticed we're avoiding each other. They're worried that there's a problem with the agency."

"But I assume you assured her there wasn't." He seemed so calm and complacent, so unlike himself that Tess moved even closer.

"Yes. I assured her, but I think she has a point. We need to stop avoiding each other."

Blake rubbed his left temple. "Tess, I'm not avoiding you. I'm busy."

He did look tired, and without considering the wisdom of her actions, she started to circle his desk.

"What are you doing?" he asked when she was a couple of feet away from him.

What was she doing? Good question. "I thought I'd give you a neck rub," she said lamely, realizing what a stupid idea it was even as she said it. "Never mind."

"Yeah, never mind. I think we'll be a lot better off if we don't rub each other's body parts, don't you?"

She quickly moved back to the other side of his desk, feeling a flush climb her cheeks. Where was her common sense? Of course she shouldn't touch him. "Good point. Sorry."

"So, is that all you came to talk to me about? You want me to stop avoiding you." His tone was flat, but there was something in his eyes that caught her attention. Something wild. Something undeniably male. His look made shivers of awareness dance across her skin.

Finding her voice proved difficult, but eventually she said, "I think it would be good if the employees saw us together."

Slowly, by teasing degrees, a grin crossed his face. That grin made her heart pound and desire race through her body. "Sure, Tess. No problem. If you want, I'll shadow you wherever you go. I'll even loiter around the ladies' room door. It won't make the employees stop talking about us, but at least it will give them something different to worry about."

His humor helped lighten the sensual mood settling around them. "That should help. Now they'll only worry about you being a pervert, not about us avoiding each other."

When his gaze met hers, she couldn't look away. The connection between them was strong and getting stronger with each passing day. They still had at least four trips to make together, and Tess didn't know if her nerves could take much more. The attraction she felt to him was like an undertow—strong, relentless. The more she willed her body to stop wanting him, the more she wanted him.

It was annoying. And confusing.

"All set for Charleston tomorrow?" he asked, his gaze still locked with hers.

"Yes. And I can only hope we find someone half as photogenic as Alex. His shots are wonderful. Did Annie show you?"

As she watched, Blake's eyes darkened. Then, abruptly, he blinked and looked away, shattering the mood. "Yes. I saw the photos. They're good. Women ought to be lined up around the block after they see Tyler and Alex. Great campaign, Tess."

His compliment caught her off guard and made her unexpectedly pleased. She was proud of the way the ads were turning out. "Thanks."

Blake stood. "I don't mean to be rude, but I have a lot of work I need to do if I'm going to find the extra time to shadow you. I'll walk you back to your office now, and on the way, we'll go by everyone's desk so they can see me stalking you."

Tess couldn't prevent herself from laughing softly. "You're completely insane."

Blake crossed the room and took her arm. When he smiled down at her, small crinkles fanned out from his gorgeous blue eyes. Tess's breath caught in her throat. For one heartbeat, she thought he would close the few inches between them and kiss her. But he didn't. And she told herself she was glad he didn't.

"Come on, Tess, let me walk you back to your office so I can get some work done."

She nodded absently, her attention still riveted on his handsome face. Reluctant to move away from him just yet, she said, "Did I tell you I have a lead on a possible Loverboy in Charleston?"

"Now there's something women don't say to me every day."

She smiled, which wasn't easy since he still loosely held her arm. His touch was warm, and it made her feel flushed all over. She longed to feel him touch much, much more than just her arm. But that kind of thinking could only lead to trouble.

Forcing her thoughts back to business, she explained, "My roommate from college, Megan Bryant, is meeting us at the local animal shelter she and her husband run. She says there's a volunteer there who would be perfect. He's studying to be a vet, and Megan claims he's sweet and very handsome."

"Sounds like Megan has a crush on this guy."

Tess shook her head. "No way. Megan's been married for almost ten years to her high-school sweetheart. Her marriage is one of those truly happy ones. Anyway, I told her we'd stop by the shelter tomorrow after we check into the hotel."

Idly, Blake's fingers stroked her arm, and Tess sucked in a tight breath. She wanted him so much. With more willpower than she knew she possessed, she took a step away from him, away from the temptation he posed.

Blake dropped his hand immediately. "Sounds good. Maybe this trip will be a short one. I can use the extra time. I'm looking into finding a loan or an investor."

Tess had intended on leaving his office, but his words stopped her cold. "You're already looking for someone to buy me out?"

"These things take time. If you want out of the agency after we finish the Loverboy campaign, I need to locate investors now."

Tess knew he was right. It would take some time to find the right person or group to buy her share of the business. But it felt odd knowing that soon she'd be out of here, no longer part of Blake's life.

Still, this was the right thing to do. She didn't belong in an ad agency. Even though she'd had a couple of good ideas on the Loverboy campaign, it wasn't what she was trained for. She spent a large part of each day trying to figure out what she was doing.

"I hope you have luck," she said. Before she could add anything else, Molly buzzed in.

"Call for you on line one. It's Stephanie Collins."

If memory served Tess right, Stephanie and Blake had been hot and heavy a couple of years ago. She seemed to remember Jason telling her once that Blake was dating one of the top ten richest women in Chicago.

"Steph and her father invest in small businesses, so I gave her a call to see if they're interested in D&S," Blake told her.

Tess had no doubt that Stephanie Collins was interested in D&S. More specifically, she was interested in one of the owners.

"That's a really friendly breakup," Tess said, trying to push away the jealousy she felt. Stephanie Collins was smart and gorgeous. Exactly the right sort of woman for Blake.

"Sure, it was friendly. She wanted marriage. I didn't."

"Has she gotten married since you broke up?"

Blake frowned. "Don't go there, Tess. She isn't interested in getting back together. This is just business."

"If you say so." Sheesh, and he called her naïve. Tess would bet her laptop computer that Steph was hoping to rekindle an old flame. But it wasn't her problem. Blake wasn't hers. If he wanted to approach an old girlfriend for money, fine. She wouldn't be part of the agency after he got the money, so what did she care if he took the money from Stephanie Collins and her father?

So if it had nothing to do with her, why did she feel like her insides were tied in knots? She glanced at Blake, who gave her a questioning look.

"I need to take this call, Tess. Are we done?" he asked even as he headed back to his desk.

Oh, yeah. They were done.

"JAMAL'S OVER HERE. I didn't tell him a word about your ad campaign, but he'll be perfect," Megan Bryant said as she led Blake and Tess between the rows of cages. Blake followed the two women, but his mind wasn't on this trip at all.

This thing with Tess was getting out of hand. Yesterday, he'd had second thoughts about approaching Steph and her father for funding. How stupid was that? Steph's dad was a great guy. He wouldn't interfere. He'd let Blake run the agency the way he saw fit.

But he hadn't asked Steph simply because of the look Tess had given him. That damn wounded puppy look had made him feel guilty for approaching an old girlfriend. He'd ended up simply telling Steph about the agency and letting her believe the only reason he'd called was to find out if any of their companies were interested in expanding their advertising. A couple were interested, so the irony was he'd set up two more meetings with prospective clients, but he hadn't secured venture capital.

"These kittens are so cute," cooed Tess as she glanced in a cage.

Blake stopped next to her and looked at the kittens. There were five of them, and they were mewing and tumbling all over each other. One small tabby stopped and stared right at him. A chill danced up his spine.

"Is this a no-kill facility?" he asked, causing both Megan and Tess to look at him.

Megan was a very perky redhead, who along with her husband, Tim, ran the animal shelter. "Yes, we are at the moment. And if our fundraiser tomorrow night goes well, we can continue to be no-kill. But running this place costs a lot of money, so we spend most of our time asking for help."

"You're having a fundraiser?" Tess asked.

Megan nodded. "Yes. It's a big deal, down at the Ward hotel. Very ritzy. We're hoping to make tons of money." She glanced at Tess, then at Blake, and a grin appeared on her face. "I have a great idea. Why don't you two come to the fundraiser? There'll be food and dancing and very few speeches. Please come. Tim would love to meet you, Blake."

Blake looked at Tess. Personally, he could think of about a thousand reasons for them not to stick around Charleston if Jamal worked out. But Megan was Tess's friend. She'd probably welcome the chance to stay here for a couple of days.

"I don't know," Tess said, her gaze brushing over Blake before returning to her friend.

"Oh, come on." Megan smiled at both of them. "Even if Jamal says yes, don't you need some time to get all the paperwork done?"

This was obviously important to Tess's friend, and she was right, they certainly would have enough details to work out with Jamal to justify spending another day here. Blake decided to make things easy for Tess.

"Why don't we stay, Tess? We both could use a day off."

Tess looked at him, a wealth of concern in her expression. "I'm not sure."

"It will be okay," Blake assured her. Surely by now she knew he wasn't going to make another move on her. The kiss had been a one-time thing. It was history. To drive his point home that she was perfectly safe with him, he did the only thing he could think of. He went cross-eyed.

A laugh burst out of Tess. "Fine. We'll stay."

"Good." Megan turned and led them to the back exit of the shelter. When they got outside, they walked over to a young man exercising a group of dogs.

"Jamal Thomas, I'd like you to meet my friend Tess Denison and her partner, Blake Sutherland," Megan said.

One look at the young man was enough. Tess flashed a triumphant grin at Blake, and he agreed with her. If Jamal Thomas wanted to do the ads, then they'd found their third Loverboy.

"Megan said you were coming for a visit." Jamal smiled at both of them. "It's nice to meet you."

Blake stepped forward and shook Jamal's hand. "It's nice to meet you, too. But Tess and I have a different reason for being here other than a visit. Got a minute?"

With a bemused expression, Jamal nodded. "Sure."

Blake and Tess outlined the Loverboy campaign for him. Jamal had a few questions, but he definitely was interested. Since Megan and Tess were friends, the young man didn't have a lot of reservations. Within thirty minutes, they'd ironed out the preliminary details.

"We'll be in touch," Blake told Jamal, shaking his hand and thanking him for agreeing. "You'll have fun."

Jamal smiled. "Yeah. I think having my face in magazines and on billboards will rock. Thanks for asking me."

"Thanks for saying yes," Blake said. "You made this trip easy."

As Tess and Blake were leaving, Megan said, "I'm sorry I can't have dinner with you tonight, but Tim and I are having dinner with his parents. The fundraiser tomorrow night should be a blast, though."

Tess gave her friend a hug. "We'll be fine. We can entertain ourselves. I can't tell you how much I appreciate you finding Jamal. He's going to be terrific."

"Honey, any time you need me to find good-looking young men, just let me know. Tim might not be too thrilled, but hey, I'm willing to make the sacrifice for my friend."

Tess laughed. "Thanks."

Megan winked at her, then looked with open speculation at Blake. "Of course, it looks to me like you've already got a handsome man."

Megan's remark surprised Blake. She'd obviously noticed the tension between the two of them, but she'd put the wrong spin on it.

Tess looked at him briefly, then back at her friend. "Megan, it's not like that."

To save Tess any awkwardness, he moved away to

let the women talk. A cage near the front door caught his attention, so he went over and looked inside. Four brown and black puppies were yapping, so full of life and energy it was impossible not to smile.

One of the things he hated about apartment living was that he couldn't have a dog. He glanced at Tess and Megan, and since they were involved in an intense conversation—no doubt about him—he knelt next to the cage and patted the pups.

"Ah-ha, a dog man. I knew it," Megan said when she came over to stand next to him. "Don't suppose you want to adopt the whole litter."

For one minute, Blake wished he could say yes. Growing up, he would have given anything to own a dog. But money had been tight, and pets cost money.

"I wish I could," he told Megan. "But for starters, I live in Chicago, not here. Plus, my apartment complex doesn't allow pets. Just as well. I travel so much a dog would get lonely."

Tess moved forward. Her soft expression made him feel self-conscious but he refused to look away. "I didn't know you liked dogs," she said.

Ah, hell. The look on her face made it clear he'd earned brownie points for liking animals. He didn't want to soften her opinion of him. He was much better off with Tess keeping her distance.

"I don't like all dogs," he said, hoping to undo some of the damage. "In fact, there are lots of dogs I don't like. Little dogs. Fancy dogs. Anything that looks good in a bow."

Tess was still giving him sweet looks when she said, "No toy poodles for you."

"A guy's got to have his standards."

Out of the corner of his eye, Blake watched Megan assess them. When she looked at Tess, she had a knowing grin on her face.

"Hey, Blake," Megan started. "Maybe when you get back to Chicago, you can look for a new place to live. Someplace that allows dogs. Or better yet, maybe you could move into a house that has a backyard. That's the kind of place you need. A house with a big backyard."

"Maybe," he said, not certain where Megan was going with this.

Megan's expression was too smug for words as she looked at Tess and added, "You know who has a house? Tess." She grinned. "And if memory serves me, it has a big backyard. It's the perfect place for a guy and his dog."

6

"YOU LOOK LIKE SIN in high heels," Megan said, spinning Tess around. "Wait until the guys get a load of you. They're going to need CPR."

Tess looked at herself in the hotel mirror, uncertain how she felt about the end result. Maybe she should have simply gone out and bought a dress for the fundraiser rather than agreeing to borrow one of Megan's. This slinky black dress was made for Megan's svelte body. On Tess, it clung to her curves, making her look...like sin in high heels.

"Seriously, you look amazing." Megan fiddled with Tess's hair, which they'd left loose and curled to fluff around her face and drape down her back. "You have such pretty hair. You shouldn't wear it in a bun. You should always leave it loose."

"It gets in my way," Tess said, spinning a little, still unable to believe her reflection in the mirror.

Megan frowned at her. "Then wear clips to keep it out of your face. Do what you have to do, but don't hide it anymore. Guys love long hair."

"I'm not interested in attracting guys," Tess maintained.

Megan's only response to that statement was a huff. She continued to fuss with Tess's dress and makeup until she finally declared her done. "No one is going to recognize you, sweetie. Tim hasn't seen you in three years. He won't know it's you. And Blake's going to forget how to speak."

Tess finished applying shimmering cranberry lipstick and looked at Megan. "Don't start."

Megan rested her hands on her hips and gave Tess an innocent look. "Don't start what?"

"Don't try shoving me at Blake. I told you, we're business partners, that's all. And before you deny matchmaking, you were doing it yesterday at the animal shelter."

Megan helped Tess put on a gold necklace. "You're no fun. What's the point in working with a guy like Blake if you're not going to seduce him? If I weren't married, I'd be chasing Blake around this hotel room."

Before Tess could say anything, Megan headed across the room and rummaged through her purse, "Which reminds me. You need these."

Tess wandered over, stumbling to a stop when she saw what her friend had in her hand. "Holy cow, Megan, those are condoms. I don't need condoms."

Megan rolled her eyes and tossed the condoms into the drawer of the bedside table. "You never know."

Drawing in a deep breath, Tess faced her friend. She knew Megan meant well, but the woman was way off track here. "I'm not going to get involved with Blake."

Megan grinned. "Okay. Fine by me if you don't want to have a long-term relationship with him. But you two are here tonight, and you do look like sin.

Something wicked might happen. If you're lucky. Hence the condoms."

A braver woman would argue, but Tess didn't see the point. Megan would believe what she wanted to believe.

"We're going to be late if we don't get going," Tess said, grabbing her purse and tugging Megan toward the door. "Let's go meet the guys."

But as she and Megan rode down in the elevator, Tess felt her stomach tie in knots. She did look different tonight, not at all like her usual self. What would Blake think when he saw her? Would he agree with Megan that she looked like sin? Would he care?

The odd thing about Blake was he seemed to be attracted to her even when she wasn't dressed up. He'd kissed her in Dallas when she'd been wearing her most conservative suit. Was that because Blake flirted with all women, regardless of what they looked like?

Tess didn't like that thought at all, so she pushed it away. Tonight was about enjoying herself. She was with one of her closest friends. She looked great. She felt great. For just one night, she could forget about the agency and the future. She could—and she would—enjoy herself.

After the elevator reached the ground floor, Tess and Megan headed to the bar to meet Blake and Tim. They found the men watching baseball on the wide-screen TV.

Tim spotted them first. He was a tall man with thinning brown hair, and his quiet personality was the perfect foil to Megan's exuberant one.

"Hi, Tess," he said, moving forward and sliding one arm around his wife's waist. "You both look pretty tonight."

Megan dropped a kiss on her husband's cheek. "Thank you, dear. I'll agree, Tess is gorgeous. No frumpy suits or sensible shoes for her tonight. She's going to be the sexiest woman at the party. Don't you think so, Blake?"

Tess groaned at her friend's obvious attempt at matchmaking. Turning to Blake, she started to tell him he didn't need to compliment her. But the look in his blue eyes made the words evaporate on her lips.

Fire. The look Blake was giving her was pure fire. It made the blood pound through Tess's veins, and she took a step toward him before she considered the wisdom of her action. He looked pretty good himself tonight. He had on her favorite suit, the dark blue Armani that made him look like every fantasy she'd ever had.

Oh, my.

"Tess, you look beautiful," he said, his deep voice husky. "Absolutely beautiful."

There was no doubting the sincerity in his voice and in the scalding look he was giving her. She didn't want to care what Blake thought about her appearance, but she did. A lot. And knowing he thought she looked beautiful made her feel that way.

"Thank you. You look pretty good yourself."

Blake chuckled and winked at her. "I bet you say that to all the guys."

When he reached down and took her hand, Tess's

heart slammed against her ribs. This was bad. Very bad. There were reasons why she and Blake shouldn't get involved. Good reasons based on logic. But at the moment, she couldn't think of a blasted one.

Blake dipped his head and said softly near her ear, "You really do look gorgeous. But I kind of like your schoolmarm look, too. It gets my blood pumping."

Tess didn't know whether to laugh or kiss him. "Oh, right, my normal look is so breathtaking."

"I think so."

Leaning back, Tess met his gaze. He couldn't really like her conservative clothes, could he? But the half smile he gave her made her believe him. And knowing that Blake thought she was attractive even when she wasn't wearing a skimpy black evening gown made her feel...special.

"Thank you for saying that," she said.

He lightly brushed her hair back from her face. "I mean it."

"Yoo-hoo, Tess and Blake," Megan said with a laugh. "There'll be plenty of time tonight for the two of you to whisper secrets to each other. Right now we need to get in gear so we're not late."

Blake smiled at Megan and Tim, his hand still wrapped around Tess's. "Let's get doing. Tonight should be fun." When he returned his attention to Tess, her heart did a little pitter-pat. "Right, Tess?"

Tess merely nodded. Tonight was going to be fun. As she looked at Blake's handsome face with his devilish smile, she amended her opinion.

Tonight was going to be a *lot* of fun.

"YOU DIDN'T have to make that donation to the shelter," Tess said.

Blake had been watching Megan and Tim along with Jamal and his girlfriend on the dance floor, but now he turned to look at Tess. His gaze lingered on her. She looked so amazing. Hot. Vibrant. Sensual.

He wanted her. Badly.

Desire had been humming through his veins since he'd seen her at the hotel. But he hadn't been kidding Tess earlier. He found her sexy when she wore schoolmarm suits, too. And he'd give anything to see her in her white nightgown with the bluebonnets.

Mostly he'd really like to see her naked.

Wanting to hold her close again and welcoming any excuse to do so, he asked, "Would you like to dance?"

Tess shook her head. "I'd rather go for a walk. It's warm in here."

That was an understatement. It felt like a hundred degrees, especially every time Tess leaned over to talk to Megan. The movement displayed an impressive amount of cleavage.

"A walk sounds like a good idea." He stood and held her chair.

The hotel where the fundraiser was being held had an elaborate garden. Several couples already wandered the manicured paths. Blake fell into step next to Tess, hoping the night air might cool his blood. But the atmosphere was sultry, and Blake knew keeping his mind off sex wasn't going to be easy.

"So why did you do it?" Tess asked, turning to look at him.

"Do what?"

"Donate to the shelter. Just because Megan's my friend is no reason to help."

Blake stopped and looked at her. The light from one of the lamps on the path illuminated her face. Her expression was sweet, warm. All he wanted to do was shimmy her out of that dress and make crazy love with her. Drawing a deep breath into his lungs, he forced himself to look away.

"I like animals," he said. "My sister says I'm a sucker for a sad face."

"You have a sister?" Tess took a step closer to him.

"Yeah. Lisa. She's younger than I am, and is in grad school at the moment." He started to walk again, hoping to break the spell that was settling around them. They'd agreed they wouldn't kiss anymore but she wasn't making it easy. Tess was looking at him as if he'd hung the moon just because he liked animals and had a sister.

"Are you close? Do you see her a lot?" Tess's arm brushed against his, and Blake couldn't make himself move away.

"All the time."

"I think that's sweet." Her soft tone made Blake put a little distance between them.

"You wouldn't say that if you'd seen the way Lisa and I fought when we were kids. She was always embarrassing me in front of my girlfriends."

If anything, his story made the look on Tess's face turn even softer. Damn. How much was he supposed to resist? First the killer dress, now she was looking at him with a combination of admiration and desire.

"Tess, I think we should go back inside," he said, hoping to escape before he did something stupid.

But rather than heading back toward the hotel, she moved even closer to him. "You're a nice guy, Blake Sutherland."

That was it. He held her gaze and said slowly, "No. I'm not. I'm thinking all sorts of very non-nice things right now. You told me not to kiss you again, but if we stay out here, I can't make any promises. And just so you know, I want to do a hell of a lot more than just kiss you."

"You do?" Her voice had a breathless hitch to it.

Gritting his teeth, he said, "Yes, so we need to go back inside."

He watched as emotions chased across her pretty face. Finally she said, "First tell me one thing. Are you still dating Stephanie?"

Where had she gotten that idea? "No. I didn't even end up asking her to invest in D&S."

"Oh."

"Tess, I wouldn't be standing here with you if I was involved with someone else. For the record, it's been a long time since I've had a lady in my life."

She gave him a small smile that made lust settle low in his body.

"In that case, what if I feel the same way you do?" She tipped her head, studying him. "What if I'd like to do more than just kiss you?"

Blake felt the air leave his lungs in a big whoosh. He

hadn't expected this. "Do you think that's smart? I thought we agreed having an affair is risky."

"I know. Having an affair is risky," she admitted. "But we're not going to work together for much longer. You're already looking for investors. Soon, I won't be part of D&S."

He couldn't believe they were really considering getting involved. "You need to know, I'm not interested in settling down."

She drew in a deep breath, almost as if she were storing up her resolve. "I'm not looking for anything long-term, either. After you buy me out, I'll need to start a new career. I won't have time for a relationship." She took a step toward him. "I think we both want the same thing, especially tonight."

Hey, whose side was she on? Tess didn't strike him as the casual-affair type. "I'm not sure we want the same thing. I want to pull you back inside so you can tell your friends goodbye and we can get back to the hotel. After that, I want to find the nearest bed and not leave it for two days."

He reached out and gently trailed his fingers down the side of her face. Need made his voice husky as he said, "I want to make love to you in every way I can think of. I want to hear you scream my name, then I want to drive you so crazy that you can't remember your own name. Is that the sort of thing you have in mind?"

Blake's heart thumped wildly in his chest while he waited for her answer. For several long moments, they looked at each other. All he could think about was kissing Tess.

A smart man would take her back to the hotel, say good-night, and head off to his own room before things went too far. A smart man would recognize danger when he saw it standing directly in front of him.

So maybe he wasn't very smart after all. Because when Tess breathed the word "yes," he slowly leaned toward her, and his last thought before their lips met was that maybe neither of them was very smart.

TESS HADN'T REALIZED how much she wanted to kiss Blake again until his lips met hers. The feeling of rightness was instantaneous. Overwhelming. This was what she'd longed for, what she'd craved for so many weeks.

Especially today. All day, she'd felt closer to him than she had to another person in a long, long time. He'd been fun and entertaining while they'd toured the historic district of Charleston.

But it was more than that. Over the last few weeks she'd come to trust Blake. When Jason had disappeared, he'd stayed. And together, they were saving the agency and their investments. She admired him for toughing it out. Admired him for the way he treated the people around him. Blake was turning out to be completely different from what she'd expected. She'd always thought he was a man like her brother or her father. A man who only cared about himself. But he was so much more. And tonight, as he looked at her with desire in his eyes, he was irresistible.

What harm could it do to give in to the need they both felt? They were adults, unattached. Shouldn't she just once get the chance to make love with a man who drove her wild? Why did her life always have to be tame?

When he brushed his lips against hers, lust zapped through her, and she knew she was doing the right thing. She wanted to be with Blake, to experience everything with him. Almost without thinking, her arms drifted up to slide around his neck, pulling him closer. She'd never felt this tempted before, but she wanted this man. This funny, sexy, kind man.

Heat flamed through her as he slid his tongue across her bottom lip. She parted her lips, and his tongue entered her mouth. She felt as if a hand wrapped around her heart and squeezed. Slowly, with languorous caresses, he explored her mouth, and then coaxed her own tongue into a gliding rhythm.

Sanity was replaced by need. Raw, primitive need. She shifted closer. "Blake," she breathed when he eventually broke the kiss to place his lips on her forehead.

"We can't do this here," he said softly as he looked into her eyes. "Do you want to go back to the hotel?"

She knew what he was doing. He was giving her another chance to change her mind. She didn't hesitate. "Yes."

"Okay." He took her hand and wrapped his fingers around hers. Then with a gentle tug, he half pulled her through the garden and into the hotel. They first found Jamal and his girlfriend, followed quickly by Megan and Tim. After a hasty goodnight, they grabbed a cab and headed back to their own hotel. On the way, Blake kissed her time and again. Slow, deep kisses that made her warm, and weak, and ready.

"Tess, you're driving me insane." His voice was husky, and when she wrapped her arms even more tightly around him, he groaned into her open mouth. Tess knew how he felt, especially when he cupped her face and proceeded to kiss her as if she held the key to paradise.

The man tasted like heaven and felt like sin. She caressed his shoulders, enjoying the feel of his muscles. Her own boldness surprised her, but she hungered for him.

They arrived at their hotel none too soon for Tess. Without comment, Blake paid the cabdriver and they both quickly made their way across the lobby. In the elevator, Blake held her hand securely, his thumb lightly brushing her palm. For a brief moment, second thoughts tried to crowd into Tess's mind, but she refused to listen to them. Tonight with Blake didn't mean anything, and she'd make certain it didn't change anything. For once, she wanted to be reckless, wanted to experience heat and fire, lust and madness.

"You're really sure about this?" Blake asked her once again when they stood outside her hotel room door.

Tess laughed softly. "You just don't take yes for an answer, do you?"

To convince him, she pushed open the door to her room, and pulled him inside. This was her night, her night to be the type of woman she'd never allowed herself to be until now. Blake's desire empowered her, and she wanted to explore all the wicked possibilities his kiss promised.

When he kissed her again, she tipped her head to taste him better and slid her tongue along the inside of his bottom lip. When his tongue met hers, need jolted through her with straining urgency, and when he pressed against her, she groaned.

"Make love to me, Blake," she whispered.

He grinned. "My pleasure."

BLAKE COULDN'T REMEMBER the last time desire had clawed at him this way. Tess made him wild. Frantic. He wanted to take her right here, right now. Up against the door. Fast and hard. Then later on the bed, slow and soft. Any way and every way possible.

But he couldn't do that until he knew for a fact that she understood this frenzy wouldn't lead anywhere except to sex. He wasn't going to propose tomorrow. There would be no orange blossoms and diamond rings.

Lifting his head, he held her gaze, studying her darkened eyes for the slightest hint of reluctance, but there was none. Still, he tried once more to bring sanity into the picture.

"Tess, you really understand that I'm not interested in settling down, in getting married. I can't promise you anything." He drew a ragged breath into his lungs. "I can't offer you anything. Tell me one last time you understand."

Impatiently, he waited for her response, bracing himself for her reaction, knowing there was every chance she'd tell him she'd changed her mind. But he'd take that chance. He wouldn't take advantage of her. If Tess had sex with him tonight, she had to know it was nothing more than quenching a physical need.

"I wasn't planning on asking you to marry me," Tess teased, a tempting smile on her face. "Unless you feel I'm going to take advantage of you."

He chuckled. "I'm definitely counting on you taking advantage of me."

Her soft laugh was more of a sigh. "Good. Because that's exactly what I intend on doing." She trailed one hand up the side of his neck, settling it on his shoulder. "You know, I can honestly say I've never had sex so good it made me forget my own name. But I like the idea." She ran one finger down his cheek and across his lips. "Very much. Do you think you can make good on that promise?"

Blake had never been so certain of anything in his life. "Absolutely."

She grinned and stood on her toes to kiss him. He pulled her against him so she could feel how aroused she made him. When she rubbed rhythmically against him, a low moan escaped his lips.

Blood pounded through his veins, and Blake gave in to the need to touch her. The curve of her back. The swell of one hip. The softness of a breast. He thumbed her nipple through her slinky dress. Tess broke the kiss—with effort since he didn't want it to end—and took his hand.

"The bed is this way," she said.

"Glad you know where it is, because I think I've lost my sense of direction." He dropped a couple of kisses on her neck. "Guess I'll have to feel my way around."

Tess laughed as she reached over to turn off the light by the bed.

"No way. I want to see you," he said, stopping her. He wanted to see her body, to look into her eyes when he entered her, to watch her beautiful face when she climaxed. He couldn't remember ever feeling this way about a woman, so attuned to her desires, but he refused to analyze his emotions right now. This wasn't the time to think about anything except pleasure.

He watched indecision cross her face. "I'm not as beautiful as the women you're used to."

Blake shook his head. "No. You're more beautiful. Can't you tell how much I want you?"

He tried to kiss Tess again, but she stopped him by placing one small hand on his chest. She studied him, her gaze intent. Whatever she saw in his eyes must have convinced her that he was sincere. After a brief hesitation, she moved back a couple of steps.

"I've always had this little fantasy." She smiled a sexy little smile that had just a touch of uncertainty. "Do you have any interest in fantasies, Blake?"

He was pretty certain his heart stopped beating for a moment. "I'm game for whatever you have in mind. You make this evening perfect for you, sweetheart."

"Okay." She drew in a deep breath, then unzipped her slinky dress. With only the tiniest hesitation, she pushed the dress off. It fell into a shiny puddle at her feet.

"You next." Her words were a mere whisper in the silence of the room.

Blake felt lust pound hard and heavy through him as he looked at her. Her bra and panties were conservative, but black. He loved black underwear. As much as he wanted to rush her, he had to let her do this her way. He wanted tonight to be everything Tess had ever imagined. For his part, he wanted to savor every second, every caress and sigh.

"Sure." He took off his jacket and draped it over a chair, his gaze lingering on Tess. She looked so beautiful, so perfect, that he fumbled as he unbuttoned his shirt. Finally, he managed to get it off. He tossed it on the chair with his jacket. When he looked back at Tess, her attention was firmly focused on his chest. She took a half step toward him, then stopped.

Tess's gaze finally met his, her expression apologetic. "Sorry to stare. You're so...um..." She waved one hand at his chest. "I mean you're so—"

He chuckled. Despite never being so aroused in his life, he couldn't resist teasing her. "Amazing? Phenomenal? Awe-inspiring?"

Her smile was pure mischief. "Yes. To all three." She nodded at his suit pants. "It's still your turn."

"Jeez, are you always this bossy?" He teased as he unzipped his pants. Anxious to end this game, he took off his shoes and socks at the same time he shucked his pants. He stood before her in his boxers and raised an eyebrow. "Remember these?"

Tess didn't answer immediately. She appeared to be one hundred percent focused on his black boxers with the little red kisses all over them.

"Did you wear those for me?" she asked.

"Yes."

This time when she smiled, it was sweet. "Thank you."

"You may not feel that way when you learn I fully expect you to put on your white nightgown at some point tonight. Then I'm going to take it off you with my teeth."

A dull flush climbed Tess's chest and face, but rather than looking embarrassed, she looked aroused.

He studied her practical bra that covered her breasts completely. He wasn't certain how much more he could take. Tess made him hot, burning hot. He hungered for her, desperate to touch her soft skin, taste her sweet mouth.

"I'm pretty sure it's your turn," he said, his voice raspy with need.

"Um, okay." When she reached behind her to the catch on her bra, Blake sucked in a tight breath, waiting. There was just enough hesitation in her movements that he knew being this forthright about sex was new to her. The fact that she trusted him enough to explore her fantasy with him made him feel humble.

Finally, with agonizing slowness, she unhooked the bra, then drew the straps down her arms. She looked at him right before she pulled the fabric away. For a fraction of a second, he saw uncertainty in her hazel eyes.

Then she let her bra drop to the floor.

Blake didn't mean to stare, but he couldn't help himself. She was so...perfect. Full, firm breasts, pretty pink nipples that were now hard and begging to be suckled. He groaned.

"Is that a good groan or a bad groan?" Tess asked.

Blake grinned. "Honey, that's an I've-died-and-gone-to-heaven groan."

She flashed a tiny smile again, obviously pleased. A fragment of emotion tugged at him. He couldn't pretend this woman didn't get to him. Of course he felt something for Tess. He liked and respected her. But that was it. That was all he felt. Still, he intended on spending most of the night both telling and showing Tess how desirable she was.

Deciding to speed up this little peek-show game, he pulled off his boxers and walked over to her. "Is it just me, or is it hot in here?" he murmured as he placed his hands on her waist.

She tipped up her head and looked at him. Her skin was flushed and soft. "It is definitely hot in here."

Murmuring a hasty apology, he helped her slip off her panties. Once they were both naked, he skimmed one hand down her body and between her legs. She was warm and wet and more than ready for him. Sliding one finger inside her, he watched her eyes darken with lust.

"I'm through playing games. Now it's time to get serious," he said, capturing her lips in a searing kiss.

7

TESS WAS POSITIVE nothing could feel better than what Blake was doing to her body. He kept bringing her to the edge, then pulling back just as she was about to fall. But as much as she adored his caresses, if he didn't stop soon, she was going to scream with frustration.

"Blake, please," she murmured against his mouth.

He broke the kiss, his gaze locked on hers as he increased the rhythm of his hand, subtly changing the pressure. Tess clung to him, struggling to catch her breath as she shattered in his arms.

"Wow," she said, once she could think again. She probably should be embarrassed by what had just happened, but she couldn't be. Not while Blake looked at her with a combination of lust and tenderness.

Blake chuckled deep in his chest. "Glad you liked it."

"Like is an understatement," she muttered, half pulling, half pushing him over to the bed. They toppled onto the mattress, Blake catching her weight and rolling under her. He reached up, cupping her breasts, his thumbs lightly rubbing against her tight nipples. Desire shot through Tess, pooling between her legs. Feeling far more daring than she ever had before, she smiled at him, and then kissed him deeply, drawing his tongue into her mouth and sucking.

She really loved kissing Blake. He always seemed as if he couldn't get enough of her, as if she drove him as crazy as he drove her. It gave her a heady sense of power knowing she got to this strong, sexy man.

When he rolled her over onto her back, she thought he finally was going to take her, but he didn't. Instead, he shifted to her side, and propped his head up on one hand. He watched her closely as he fondled her breasts, rubbing their hardened nipples with lazy, sensuous strokes. Tess ran one hand across his chest, enjoying the sensation of the thick hair against her fingertips. Leaning up a little, she skimmed her hand down his belly and below, encircling his erection.

Blake closed his eyes as she explored him. She watched in fascination as the muscles in his jaw tensed. Finally, he reached down and gently removed her hand from around him.

"Honey, I can't wait any longer. I have condoms in my wallet." Blake made a move to get up from the bed, but Tess stopped him.

"I've got some." She reached into the nightstand drawer and pulled out one of the condoms Megan had left her.

"Tess, you devil." Blake leaned over and looked inside the drawer. Tipping his head, he shot her a teasing glance. "Wow, you planned ahead. Were you plotting all along on seducing me?"

She shook her head. "Megan gave me those."

He quirked an eyebrow and glanced back in the

drawer. "There are at least a dozen condoms in here. Are you expecting superhuman power?"

She giggled, loving the way he teased her, especially now. He made her feel special, not self-conscious.

"I expect you to do your best," she told him in a mock-stern tone.

Blake kissed her, nibbling at her lips. "Ooh, you're using your schoolmarm voice. I love it."

He grabbed a couple of extra condoms out of the drawer and tossed them on the nightstand. "Just in case," he told Tess with a wink.

Tess smiled and ran her hand across his flat abdomen. "I really admire overachievers."

He chuckled, the sound becoming more of a groan when her hand drifted even lower. "That feels wonderful. But if you keep on, we'll be done here before we even start."

He brushed her hand away and covered himself with one of the condoms. When he finished, he stretched out on his side, lying next to her again. She could see heated passion in his eyes, but when he kissed her, she felt both desire and gentleness.

"Tell me what you like." He brushed his fingertips over her nipples, causing her to arch, seeking more of his touch.

"Anything you do." Her words were breathless, filled with desire. "Anything at all."

"Tess." Her name was a whisper as he leaned over, capturing a nipple in his mouth and sucking.

Tess gasped, raising up and pushing her sensitive flesh deeper into his mouth. In breathless pleas, she begged him for more. He granted her wish, shifting his attention to her other breast, running his tongue over and around her impossibly tight nipple, then drawing her into his mouth. Again and again, she ran her hands over his shoulders, kneading the firm muscles in his back.

There were so many things she wanted him to do to her, so many things she wanted in turn to do to him. But she couldn't wait. Right now, all she wanted was to feel him deep inside her.

When his large hand slid between her thighs again, Tess took one moment to delight in how wickedly talented he was. Then, she cupped his face and said, "Now, Blake. I need you now."

"You are so beautiful." Watching her closely, he moved between her parted thighs. As he entered her, her eyes drifted closed.

"Look at me," he whispered.

She did as he asked, opening her eyes. She saw the fire burning in his gaze as she felt him stretch her, joining them slowly. Completely.

When he was fully inside her, he kissed her again. "Tess," he said, a touch of awe in his voice.

For that sweet second, she savored the sensation of them joined intimately together. Then, as she watched him, he started to move. Slowly at first, then faster, his strokes urgent, compelling. She moved with him, matching his rhythm, her own need meeting his. Making love had never felt this way, so consuming. So perfect. So right.

She wrapped her legs around Blake's hips, wanting

him deeper inside her, wanting to be part of him. Time and again, he thrust into her, muttered her name with a kind of breathless wonder.

Then suddenly, Tess's world grew still, focused, and the unbelievable pressure inside her exploded. She cried out, and a moment later, Blake called out her name one last time as he reached his own climax.

Afterward, they remained joined for timeless seconds. Finally, he raised his head and gave her a slow, sexy smile. "Quick—tell me your name?"

Tess laughed, enjoying the knowledge that she'd rocked his world as much as he'd rocked hers. "I do believe once or twice you really did make me forget my name."

Blake chuckled. "That was amazing, Tess. Truly amazing."

She agreed. As she ran one hand down the side of his face, it suddenly hit her why the experience had been so fantastic. They hadn't had sex. They'd made love. Or at least, she had, because she knew beyond a doubt that she was in love with Blake Sutherland.

Hopelessly, helplessly, perhaps even stupidly, in love with him.

She should be scared witless. But as Blake gathered her close, she couldn't feel upset or frightened. Not about what had happened, and not about what she was certain the future held. Because she loved him, she would take what he could offer and not worry about what would happen when it ended.

Besides, she already knew what would happen—she would go on. Sure, her heart would be dinged, but she'd go on. And knowing that she would feel heartache in the future wasn't going to stop her from savoring the present. Okay, so he wouldn't be with her forever. But he was with her tonight, and she was going to make certain the time they spent together was a fantasy come true.

BLAKE OPENED his eyes, taking a minute to remember where he was. Then the soft bump of a warm body next to him reminded him exactly where he was and with whom. He turned on his side, gathering Tess against him. She mumbled something, then snuggled close.

He wasn't surprised Tess was a snuggler. And, boy, did she ever snuggle. Several times during the night, she'd draped herself across and around him, rubbing him with half-asleep caresses, murmuring unintelligible phrases that made him smile.

He couldn't remember ever being with a woman who brought him so much pleasure, both while they were having sex and afterward. She even turned him on in her sleep. Leaning over, he gave in to temptation and started kissing his way down her body, relearning her shape, her scent.

He knew the exact moment she woke up, but she kept her eyes closed as he parted her thighs and kissed her intimately, laving her with his tongue. Tess's breathing became rapid, excited, and he kept tormenting her until she climaxed.

"Good morning," he said, grinning at her. "How are you?"

Tess smiled sleepily, trailing her fingers down the side of his face. "I'm wonderful, thanks to you. How are you?"

"Great, but there is something you could help me with." He leaned up and kissed her. When he finally lifted his head, he gazed into her eyes. The look she gave him was so sweet, so happy that it tugged at his heart.

"There's something I can do for you? Really? I wonder what it could be?" But even as she teased him, she reached across him to grab another condom out of the drawer. "We're partners. I'm always happy to help you with any little problem you're having."

"Hey. What do you mean *little* problem?"

Tess giggled, and the sound ran over Blake like warm rain. Boldly, she reached down and fondled him, her oh-so-talented fingers driving him to distraction.

"Oops, my mistake," she teased. "This is *not* a little problem. It's a huge problem. An enormous problem. An absolutely gigantic problem."

Blake rolled over onto his back, and pulled Tess on top of him. "Any idea how you can help me?"

She tossed her hair over one shoulder and ran her hands across his chest, her touch leaving a trail of heat on his skin. "I'll see what I can do."

What she proceeded to do was make mind-blowing love to him for the next half hour. By the time Blake could breathe somewhat normally, Tess lay next to him, almost asleep again. Idly, he rubbed her back, and she reached out and caressed his chest.

Right now, in the pale light of morning, there was no use pretending Tess wasn't wrapping herself around his heart, because she was. He cared about her. Cared deeply. But caring was a long way away from being in love. And he wasn't about to fall in love with her because Tess deserved more than he could offer. Sooner or later, she'd probably want to get married. Maybe have kids.

He wasn't interested in settling down. He'd spent most of his life taking care of people. Hell, he was still taking care of people. He already had enough responsibility to choke him.

But knowing he had no future with Tess didn't stop him from gathering her closer. Later, when she woke, he'd talk to her, find out what she wanted to do. They could continue to be lovers for a while as long as she truly understood this wasn't forever.

He ran his hand down her back, bringing her still closer. He had to let Tess decide where they went from here.

"YOU'RE LOOKING positively giddy today." Annie grinned at Tess. "Do you have a boyfriend you haven't told us about?"

Stunned, Tess glanced at the other woman. She couldn't know about Blake. And there was absolutely no way Annie could know what had happened last night. Tess hadn't told a soul, and she knew Blake wouldn't either.

That meant Annie's guess was truly just a guess.

"I'm just happy we found the third Loverboy," Tess told her. "Did you get in contact with Jamal yet?"

"Yes, I spoke with Jamal and the paperwork's under way. Now back to you. Ever since you got here from the airport, you've been practically glowing. And a few minutes ago, I heard you humming. You never hum. So what's up? What happened in Charleston?"

Tess made a mental note to herself to stop humming and glowing. If she didn't, the entire office would know she and Blake had become lovers.

"I'm not glowing. I'm sweating because I've been running around like a crazy woman since I got here. Now, don't you have some work to do?"

Annie laughed and headed to the door of Tess's office. "Fine. Be that way. I'm just glad you're happy."

After the younger woman left, Tess turned her attention back to her computer, but she couldn't concentrate. All she could think about was last night and the wonderful things Blake had made her feel. He'd wooed her body, and along the way, he'd seduced her heart.

But Blake wasn't interested in her heart. He'd been sweet this morning when he'd explained once again that he wasn't looking for a long-term relationship. And she'd assured him that neither was she.

Eventually, he'd seemed to believe her, and on the way home, he'd laughed and kissed with her on the airplane. But now that they were back in the office, back in the real world, Tess knew she had to make a decision. Continue being Blake's lover or end things here.

Almost as if he knew she was thinking about him, Blake appeared in the doorway to her office. He gave her a little half smile, one that spoke of the many secrets they'd shared the night before. Tess's heart raced as she smiled back at him.

"Hi there," he said, coming into her office and shutting the door.

As downright silly as it sounded, Tess couldn't remember a man ever saying anything so sexy to her. Maybe it was because that *hi* was now a greeting between two lovers who'd shared an incredible night together. "Hi there yourself." She glanced at the closed office door. "What's up?"

His smile turned into a full-fledged grin. "That's a bad question to ask a man."

Tess laughed. "If that's why you're here, you can go back to your own office. I'm not fooling around at work."

Blake shrugged and dropped into the chair facing her desk. "Fine by me. Deprive yourself. I don't care."

"Bunk."

He chuckled. "Yeah, it is."

For a second, she allowed herself the pleasure of simply looking at him. He was so breathtakingly male that Tess couldn't help but want him. But she'd meant what she'd said. Not here. Not at the office.

"So, if you're not here to..." She shrugged. "You know. Then why are you here?"

Blake had a twinkle in his eyes as he said, "You know? That's the best you can do. You know? I don't remember you being so shy last night."

Tess tucked some loose strands of hair behind one ear. She'd taken Megan's advice and skipped her usual bun, instead leaving her hair free today. It made her feel different, less restricted. More wild.

The same way being with Blake made her feel.

She met his gaze with her own. "I wasn't shy, and that's thanks to you. I didn't mention this to you before, but last night meant a lot to me. It was very empowering."

For a long heartbeat, he merely looked at her. She loved the way he looked at her, like he really saw her, saw her hopes and dreams along with the woman.

"Anytime you want to feel empowered, Tess, just let me know."

Gathering her courage, she asked, "Is tonight too soon?"

"That's what I wanted to talk to you about. I'm supposed to visit my mother tonight. Want to come along? Afterward, we can go back to my apartment or to your house and continue what we started last night."

His mother? He was taking her to meet his mother? Tess frowned. "I'm not sure I should—"

Blake shook his head. "Don't read anything into it, Tess, and my mother won't either. She knows we're running the agency together, and she'd like to meet you. We won't tell her we're also involved. Might give her the wrong idea."

He was right, of course. They shouldn't tell his mother about the change in their relationship any more than they should broadcast it to the rest of the office.

Neither of them had set out to keep this a secret, but for practical purposes, life would be simpler if they did.

"It's no big deal. We'll stop by, say hi, then go to dinner." He gave her a wicked grin, and in his most put-upon voice said, "After that, I'll let you seduce me if you absolutely insist."

Oh, she insisted, all right.

Thinking it over, she couldn't see what harm it could do to stop by and meet his mother.

"Sure. That sounds nice." She looked again at the closed door and restacked a group of papers on her desk. She wasn't trying to dismiss him, but if she didn't get him out of her office soon, she'd break her own rule about no fooling around at work. "I have a lot to do today. Is there anything else?"

He chuckled as he stood. "Oooh, there's that school-marm voice again. Be still my heart."

With a wink, he left her office. Tess watched him walk away and found herself smiling. Blake Sutherland was good for her, in lots of ways. He made work fun, which was surprising considering what a mess Jason had left for them. But together, they were turning things around. Calls were coming in from companies interested in their edgy campaigns. Word was getting out and Tess felt optimistic about the company's future.

She was proud of them. Both of them. Blake was excellent at advertising. But she felt like she'd been a major contributor to the Loverboy campaign. Maybe she didn't deserve quite as much credit as he kept giving her, but she had come up with the idea. An idea the client had liked.

Who would have believed it? She'd actually helped.

With the reputation they were gaining, finding financing so Blake could buy her out shouldn't be too much of a problem. The agency had a bright future in front of it. Investors would see that. Soon, maybe too soon, she could get her money out of the agency and move on to something else.

But those thoughts made her sad. She enjoyed coming to work these days. She felt as if she made a difference here. But more importantly, even before they'd become lovers, she looked forward to seeing Blake. Sure, he could drive her crazy. But he also made her feel pretty good about herself.

And she was majorly in love with him. The more she learned about him, the more she admired Blake. She was definitely going to miss him when she left the agency and he was no longer part of her life.

The thought of staying longer had occurred to her, but how would she feel a month from now or a year from now when he still didn't return her love? Seeing him day after day and knowing he didn't love her would kill her.

In true cowardly fashion, she decided not to worry about the future right now. Tonight, she got to be with Blake again. And no matter what happened in the future, these nights with him were worth it.

Oh, boy. And how.

"YOU MUST BE SO worried about your brother." Blake's mother smiled sympathetically at Tess. "I can't imagine what you're going through, not knowing where he is or even if he's okay. You're such a strong woman to be holding up the way you are. I admire you."

Blake glanced at Tess, who seemed genuinely touched by his mother's compliment. "Thank you, but there's nothing to admire," she said. "I'm used to things like this. Jason's taken off in the past, as has my father. Sort of runs in my family. At least, the males seem to enjoy it."

His mother gave Blake a questioning look, but he just shrugged. If he'd known Jason might simply disappear on him, he would have thought twice about going into business with his friend.

"Jason never disappeared in college," he said.

Tess leaned back against the couch, her attention on Kathleen. "I never thought he'd walk out on the business. The one time he did disappear, it was around the same time as one of my father's trips. For a few months there, I wondered if I'd ever see either one of them again."

Blake didn't know what to say. He glanced at his mother, who was looking at Tess with compassion in her eyes.

"You poor thing. My heart breaks for you. I can't imagine how terrified you must have been. How old were you?"

Tess seemed surprised at his mother's concern. "Oh, Mrs. Sutherland, it was no big deal. My dad disappeared a lot when Jason and I were growing up. We got so we could almost predict when he'd take off. And when he came back, he was very attentive for quite some time."

"But that doesn't make up for all the days he wasn't there," Blake said softly. He wanted to hug her and tell her it would be all right. Even though Tess maintained it didn't bother her, it had to. He felt sorry for the young woman she'd been. He felt angry at the two men who did this to her with blithe regularity.

And he was stunned that he felt her pain so deeply.

"You two look like you're settling in to feel sorry for me, but don't." Turning her attention to his mother, she added, "Besides, this time Jason didn't leave me alone. Blake and I have dealt with the problems at the agency together."

His mother grinned at Blake. "He's a good boy, isn't he?"

Blake groaned. "Jeez, Mom, don't start. The next thing I know, you'll be bringing out the baby pictures. Remember I have to work with Tess."

Kathleen patted his knee. "Don't worry, honey. I won't embarrass you, I promise. I won't show her any pictures of you as a baby, not even the one that shows your bare butt when you were two months old."

Tess laughed, her laughter growing when he shot her a mock scowl. "Oh, I can't tell you how much I'd love to see the naked picture."

Turning his full attention to Tess, Blake gave her a look that promised retribution later tonight when they were alone. If she wanted to see him naked, he was more than happy to comply.

Blake decided it was way past time he changed the subject. "Need anything done while I'm here, Mom?"

"Yes, I'm glad you asked. The faucet in the kitchen is leaking. Could you take a look at it?"

Before she'd finished speaking, Blake was on his feet. He headed out to the kitchen, took a quick look at the faucet, which was indeed dripping. This wouldn't take too long to—

What was he thinking? He'd left Tess alone with his mother. And the baby pictures.

He hustled back to the living room and found his mother grilling Tess. When she noticed him in the doorway, her questions dried up, and Kathleen clamped her mouth shut.

"Good try, Mom," Blake said with a chuckle. He shifted his attention to Tess. "Why don't you give me a hand in the kitchen?"

Devilment danced in his mother's eyes, but she pretended to be upset and frowned at him. "Well for pity's sake. This is the downside of having such a bright son. I can't get away with anything. Now how I am supposed to pump her for information if you won't leave us alone for ten minutes?"

"Sorry to spoil your fun." He glanced at Tess who looked uncertain about what to do. "Seriously, I think it will be safer for both of us if you help me in the kitchen."

"Okay." When Tess got to the kitchen, she followed him over to the sink. Bending her head, she watched the faucet drip a couple of times, then nodded. "Yes, it is indeed dripping. Now can I go talk to your mother?"

"No. You need to help me."

"I don't think so. The only way I know how to fix a dripping faucet is to call a plumber. Is that what you had in mind?"

Certain his mother couldn't see or hear them, Blake leaned close and dropped a quick but decisive kiss on her cheek. "If you think I'm about to let you gossip about me with my mother, you're crazy. She's dying to tell you about every single time I got in trouble as a kid."

Tess grinned, and he felt warmth course through him. "What an ego you have. Don't you think your mother and I have better things to talk about than you?"

"Um, no."

Tess giggled and nudged him toward the sink. "Get to work and fix that."

Unable to resist, Blake gave her one more quick kiss, this time on her lips. When he lifted his head, Tess looked at the entrance to the kitchen.

"Isn't this risky for you? Your mom could walk in at any moment, then you'd have to explain why you're kissing one of your business partners."

"Mom wouldn't be shocked, unless of course you were Jason."

Tess took a step away from him. "Still, I'm going to make certain she doesn't catch us."

He pretty much knew what her answer was going to be, but he asked the question anyway. "Just how do you plan on doing that?"

"By sitting with your mother in the living room," she said, right before she sprinted from the room.

Blake couldn't be upset. He was glad Tess wanted to know more about him. He wanted to know more about her, too. He knew her mother had died a few years ago, and that her father currently lived in New York. But he knew those things because Jason had told him.

Tess herself had told him little about her family. Learning that her father and brother thought nothing of disappearing without a word still stunned him.

He had to wonder what sort of business partner Jason was going to be. He couldn't afford to be in business with someone who didn't take the company seriously. When Jason came back, Blake intended on having a long, hard talk with him.

But right now, he had a more pressing concern. He could hear the women in the living room laughing and talking. And he didn't need to be a rocket scientist to know he was the subject of their discussion.

After quickly fixing the faucet, he washed up and headed toward the living room, where his greatest fear came to life. His mother sat next to Tess on the couch, a photo album open in front of them. Blake didn't have to ask if the pictures were of him. He knew they were.

"Showing her my bare butt, Mom?"

Kathleen shook her head slowly. "Please. Give me some credit." She pointed at one picture. "That one is of Blake on prom night. Don't you think he looks handsome in his tux? And here's one of the day he graduated from college. I bought him that suit, and if I say so myself, he looks drop-dead gorgeous in it."

Stunned, Blake stared at his mother. She was showing Tess pictures, all right. But they were pictures where he'd looked good.

His mother's sneaky plan hit him like a rock. Kathleen Sutherland should be ashamed of herself. Rather than trying to embarrass him, she was doing something much worse.

She was playing matchmaker.

Good Lord.

8

THE RINGING PHONE woke Tess with a start. She fumbled with the light, and let out a yelp when a muscled arm curled around her waist. For a millisecond, she wasn't sure where she was and with whom. Then she smiled. Oh yeah. Blake. The man who mere hours ago had her howling with pleasure. Once or twice, she'd definitely forgotten her own name.

Blake's hand fumbled on her hip, then with a completely insincere "whoops," explored even more of her anatomy.

"Can't seem to find the phone," he murmured in her ear.

Tess laughed and grabbed the phone for him. "You're a bad man," she whispered.

Blake was chuckling as he answered the phone. After a moment, he turned on the bedside light and looked at Tess.

"Yeah, hi. So Jason, where the hell are you? Tess and I have been keeping it together while you've been gone."

At the mention of her brother's name, Tess sat up, tucking the sheet under her arms. "Let me talk to him."

Blake hesitated for a minute, then with a shrug, handed over the phone.

"Jason, you're a rat. A complete, thorough rat. How dare you leave like that? What did you think would happen to the agency? How could you just take off?"

"Hello to you, too, Tess," Jason said, laughing. "My, my, my. I've been calling your house all evening, hoping to get the chance to talk to you. But you haven't been home. Imagine my surprise when I find you at Blake's house at eleven o'clock at night. Looks like a few things have changed since I've been gone."

Drat. Tess hadn't thought about the implication of her being at Blake's house this late at night. Naturally, Jason would immediately assume something was going on between them.

And, of course, it was.

But she had more important things to discuss with her half brother. "Where are you? When are you coming back?"

Jason sighed. "Tessie, it's not that simple. I'm...well, I need some more time."

Tess felt as if her head was in a vice. He needed time? For what?

"First, don't call me Tessie. Second, you need to come back to Chicago and face your life. You have responsibilities here. And you owe it to Blake and to me to come back and decide what you intend on doing about the agency."

She glanced at Blake, who gave her that sweet half smile of his she'd come to love. It was an understanding smile, a kind smile, but also, it was an oh-so-sexy smile. She smiled back at him.

But her good mood shattered like fragile crystal

when Jason started going on about how tough his life was and how difficult running the agency had proven to be.

Tess cut him off with a groan. "Don't give me that, Jason. Your life isn't tough. You've got a trust fund."

"I invested it all in the company."

"A company that could be very successful if you'd come home and work at it." She drew in a deep breath, trying to calm down. "You owe it to me and to Blake to come back. You talked us into creating D&S Advertising. You can't simply drop it in our laps and disappear."

"I didn't just disappear. I told you goodbye, and you didn't seem to have a problem with me leaving."

He had to be kidding. How could she possibly be related to this man? Aggravated beyond belief, she counted to ten, then said slowly, "Jason, you stopped by my office at the end of the day and said 'See you.' I thought you meant you'd see me the next day."

This was getting nowhere, and Tess knew it. Her brother would come back when he damn well wanted to and not a moment before. She'd lived through this game time and time again. The rules were always the same.

"Why did you call tonight? Why did you want to talk to me?" she asked, swallowing her frustration.

"I wanted to see how you were doing. How both you and Blake were doing." His voice sounded concerned but Tess didn't buy it for a moment. Jason wanted something. She knew it with absolute certainty.

"Let's try this again, and this time, why don't you

tell me the truth. Why did you call, Jason? And if you want money, you have to come home to Chicago and earn it."

"Jeez, Tess, you're being really hard-nosed about this. I would've thought you'd be in a better mood since you're having sex with Blake."

Tess rubbed her left temple. She wasn't going to discuss her love life with her brother. "Why did you call, Jason?"

"Okay, okay," he said. "I called to tell you it'll be a few more weeks before I can get back home. Some things have happened, and I need a little more time."

Tess felt like yelling. Or crying. Or simply hanging up. What was it about the men in her family that made them think acting foolishly was acceptable?

Blake patted her arm, and when she looked his way, he was watching her. She covered the mouthpiece and told him, "Jason called to tell us he's not coming back for a while longer. I'm sorry."

Tess expected him to be angry, but instead he shrugged. "We're doing okay by ourselves. He has to do what he has to do."

Blake's response caught her by surprise. Wasn't he angry? Didn't he want to tell his irresponsible friend a thing or two?

She held out the receiver. "Do you want to talk to him?"

Blake shook his head. "Just tell him I hope he's well."

Stunned, Tess put the phone back to her ear. She'd

fully expected Blake to give Jason a piece of his mind. Instead, he'd wished him well.

Figured. Once again, Jason was getting his way.

"Blake says he hopes you're well, but I'll tell you something, Jason. Blake is your friend, and you shouldn't treat him this way. Now do what you need to do so you can get back here. Can you at least give me a number where I can reach you in case of an emergency?"

Jason laughed. "Um, not really. Guess you and Blake will have to handle things on your own." The laughter left his voice as he added, "Hey, Tess. Heads up. Blake isn't the marriage and babies kind. Don't get me wrong. He's a great guy. But be careful, okay? I don't want to see you get your heart broken."

Tess felt like laughing. Her completely irresponsible brother was warning her about Blake. Talk about a black widow warning you about a scorpion.

"Don't worry about me, Jason. Worry about yourself. There's no telling what I'll do to you when you finally get back here."

And with a final laugh and a "take care," Jason was gone. Tess pushed the off button and set the phone on the nightstand.

"I'm sorry," Blake said.

Tess looked at him and felt horrible. How could Jason blithely dump all of this into their laps? She was used to this sort of treatment. Blake wasn't.

"No, I'm the one who's sorry. Jason's my brother."

"He's a grown man. And his mistakes aren't yours."

Blake was so nice. He had every right to be furious at

Jason, instead he was being understanding. If she hadn't already been in love with him, she would have fallen now.

"I just hate that he's done this to you," she said.

Blake smiled, his face illuminated only by the soft light of the bedside lamp. He looked so gorgeous, so strong and male, that Tess's heart beat faster. When his hand went to the sheet tucked under her arms, she felt her breath catch in her throat.

"Truthfully, Tess, I'm pretty happy that Jason took off. It gave me the chance to get to know you. When he was around, you and I never had a reason to talk to each other. Think about what we would have missed if we hadn't been forced to work together."

With his gaze still locked with hers, he gave the sheet one quick tug. It fluttered to her lap, and Blake let out a long, low whistle. "That's what I call a lovely sight."

Tess laughed. "Puh-lease. I'm barely a B-cup. Hardly enough to inspire wolf whistles."

Blake leaned over and kissed one taut nipple, his lips lingering with devastating effect. "I hate to disagree with you, especially since you may go all schoolmarmy on me, but you are wrong." Nudging her until she lay flat, he lightly suckled first one nipple, then the other. "You inspire a lot more than just whistles."

"Is that a fact?"

With a chuckle, Blake reached over and grabbed a condom off the nightstand. "Oh, yeah. That is a definite fact."

Tess closed her eyes, savoring the touch and feel of Blake. As he slowly made love to her, she had to admit, he was right about one thing. She was glad they'd gotten to know each other. She would always be glad they'd had this time together.

As long as she lived, she would never forget these days with Blake.

BLAKE COULDN'T remember the last time he'd had so many bad days straight in a row. Maybe right after his father had died, but not since then. The last two weeks, though, if something wasn't going wrong, it was about to.

"Tyler can't pull out of the campaign," Blake said. "He signed a contract."

Tess sat across the table from him. Drew and Annie were also in this emergency meeting. Damn. What was Tyler thinking? They'd already spent a fortune on the ads. He couldn't just drop out now.

"He said his girlfriend told him she'd break up with him if he did the ads. She doesn't want other women thinking he's available," Tess explained. "I spent over twenty minutes trying to reason with him, but he's adamant. He wants out."

This was all they needed. First the trip to Boston had taken four days longer than planned. No matter where they went, Tess couldn't find the kind of guy she wanted.

Then two of the companies that had contacted them about potential representation cancelled their meetings, claiming they wanted to go with a bigger agency.

Finally, his mother had called last night to ask him for even more money. Lisa had run into some additional expenses at school. At this rate, Blake knew it wouldn't be long until he was tapped out.

He rubbed the tense muscles in his neck, his gaze naturally drifting to Tess. She was the only good thing to happen to him during the last two weeks. Every night he spent hours making love with her. No day could be horrible if he got to spend at least a little time with her.

"Any ideas?" he asked.

Tess sighed. "He says Luanne is the woman he plans on marrying. He doesn't want her mad. I told him that she should be proud of him, but he says she doesn't see it that way. All she sees is his picture plastered on a billboard for millions of women to ogle."

"See, this is what I don't get," Annie piped in. "I'd like to know tons of other women agreed that my boyfriend was hot. For me, ogling would be a good thing."

"Too bad you're not Luanne." Tess looked at Blake. "I thought maybe you could try talking to him. He kept saying I wouldn't understand how he felt, so maybe you can convince him you do."

"Or we could just call in a few lawyers. Whether Tyler likes it or not, he signed a contract," Drew pointed out. "He posed for the photos. Desire Perfume has spent a lot of money on him. He can't simply change his mind."

Blake looked at the younger man. "I don't want to involve lawyers unless I have no other choice." For a few seconds, he turned the problem over in his mind. Then he glanced at Tess. "We leave for New Orleans the day after tomorrow. Let's swing by Dallas on our way. I think it would help if we met with Tyler in person."

Tess nodded. "We can try."

"Let's have dinner with him," Blake said. "Maybe in person, we can change his mind."

A smile slowly formed on Tess's lips. "What if we ask Luanne to join us, too? She may come around if we can address her concerns in person."

He thought about her idea. It could work. "Sure. Why not? At this point, we should try anything."

They ran through a few more administrative issues, then they all headed back to their offices. Blake grabbed his phone before he'd even sat down and called Tyler. Thankfully, the young man was home.

After letting Tyler explain once again why he'd changed his mind, Blake said, "You know, the money from Loverboy should be enough to help buy a ranch and pay for a nice wedding. But if Luanne is unhappy, then I can understand your problem."

Tyler was silent, which Blake knew was a good sign. He was thinking things over.

"I know you can sue me if I back out of the ads, but I can't lose Luanne. She means everything to me. I really love her," Tyler said.

Although love wasn't something Blake personally believed in, Tyler seemed genuinely upset.

"Tell me one thing. How do *you* feel about the Loverboy ad?" Blake asked. "You've seen what it's going to look like. Do you like it?"

"I think it's great," Tyler said.

That's what Blake wanted to hear. They weren't

dead yet. "Tell you what, Tyler. Tess and I have to be in your area on Wednesday. Mind if we take you to dinner? We'd also like the chance to meet Luanne. Would that work for you?"

"Sure. Sounds like a good idea. Maybe if Luanne met you two, she'd understand that you're selling cologne, not selling me."

"Exactly. Tess and I'll be happy to answer any questions she might have about the ads or the product."

He could practically hear the grin on Tyler's face. "And I can remind her how the money from the ads will make it possible for us to get married sooner."

"Sounds like a plan." Blake then made arrangements to take Tyler and Luanne to dinner in two days.

Well, he might not have put out the fire with Tyler, but he'd at least cooled it down a little. That left only a couple of other problems to address. First, he needed to spend what time he had at the office today looking into finding additional clients so the business could grow. Then he needed to talk to Lisa and find out what was going on with her. Sure, college was expensive, but not this expensive.

He rubbed the tense muscles in his neck again, but the knots refused to go away.

"You know, you once told me you thought it wasn't a good idea if we rubbed each other's body parts," Tess said as she walked into his office, closing the door behind her. "But I figure since then, our relationship has changed. Mind if I try to loosen those muscles in your neck?"

Blake smiled, happier than he had a right to be that she was here. "Feel free to rub anything you want."

Tess gave him one her famous disapproving looks, but he knew she didn't mean it. There was a definite twinkle in her eyes.

"I'll give you a massage as long as you promise to be on your very best behavior. Naturally, I realize your best behavior is still pretty wicked. But do what you can."

Blake chuckled, stunned that with just a little teasing Tess had lifted the bad mood settling around him. She affected him that way. Just being near her made him happy.

"I'll try," he promised.

Tess walked around his desk and stopped behind him. Slowly, she rubbed his shoulders and neck, kneading the knotted muscles. Blake closed his eyes and sighed. "That feels wonderful."

"Better than sex?" Tess whispered near his left ear.

"Not even close." He swiveled in his chair far enough that he could loop one arm around her waist. Before she could do much more than say "Hey," he tugged her down into his lap.

"This isn't fair. You promised you'd behave," she pointed out. But at the same time she was protesting, she also was settling into a more comfortable position in his lap. Not that comfort was what he was feeling at the moment. With Tess snuggled up against him, his tension and frustration had been replaced by fire and lust.

"You know what a liar I am." He nibbled on her

neck. "I can't be trusted, especially not when there's a pretty woman around me."

"I'd trust you with my life," Tess said softly.

Blake looked into her eyes and saw that she meant what she'd said. She really trusted him, and he knew that after growing up around her father and Jason, Tess didn't trust many people. Certainly not many men.

But she trusted him with her life.

Emotions he couldn't even name wrapped around him, making him even more confused than he already was.

"Tess, I don't know—"

"Shh. Someone very wise once told me your head can actually explode if you think too hard."

With a sexy half smile, she slid one arm around his neck and tugged him down for a long, deep kiss. He returned her kiss, showing her with his lips and his hands what she did to him.

And she did so many sweet, wonderful, crazy things to him. Soon, he needed to take the time to understand what he felt for Tess. But he couldn't sort through those feelings right now. Not when so many things were up in the air.

But soon, very soon, he'd decide what to do about Tess.

"I CAN'T STAND the thought of hundreds, heck probably thousands, of women staring at pictures of my Tyler. He's mine, and not available," Luanne said for about the fifth time. "I don't think he should be put on display."

Tess nodded thoughtfully at the other woman. So far, this dinner with Tyler and Luanne wasn't going well. Luanne was adamant that she didn't want her boyfriend posing in the ads. But the evening was still young. They'd just arrived at the restaurant thirty minutes ago. So far, she and Blake had tried to address Luanne's concerns, but they weren't having a lot of luck.

Truthfully, Tess knew part of the problem was she didn't really understand Luanne's concerns. But she was trying. She was really trying. On the flight here, she and Blake had come up with all sorts of solid selling points to present to the other woman.

But most of their solid arguments weren't cutting it with Luanne. Part of the reason was she was so young. She'd turned twenty-one a few months ago. Tess could barely remember ever being that young, but she needed to think of something to say and she needed to think of it soon. Tess mentally thumbed through the list of arguments and pulled out one of her favorites.

"Luanne, no one will know Tyler's complete name," Tess explained. "They won't be able to look him up and find out one way or the other whether he's available or not, so it won't matter."

Luanne frowned. "It will matter to me. How would you like it if I told you that I thought your boyfriend, Mr. Sutherland, is gorgeous? Wouldn't that make you mad?"

Surprised, Tess glanced at Blake, then back at

Luanne. The question didn't bother her. What did was that Luanne knew that she and Blake were involved. They were always very careful not to be anything but completely professional when they were around other people.

"Blake and I aren't—"

Luanne snorted. "Of course you are. It's written all over both of you. You two are in love. I know because Tyler and I are in love, too."

"Luanne, Tess and I are business partners," Blake said.

Luanne waved her hand, dismissing his words. "No offense, but my mama didn't raise a fool. You two are a lot more than business partners. I can tell by the way you look at each other." She shot a pointed look at Tess. "So, tell me how you'd feel if other women sat around looking at Blake and thinking how hot he is."

Rather than giving Luanne a pat answer, Tess seriously considered the question. "Honestly, it wouldn't bother me. I know Blake is very handsome. I expect other women to notice that."

"How can it not bother you? These women would be thinking sex thoughts about your man." Luanne nudged Tyler. "I couldn't stand them thinking about Tyler that way."

Blake started to say something, but Tess shook her head slightly. This was a woman-to-woman thing.

"I'm serious, Luanne, it wouldn't bother me. You know why? Because I trust Blake. He wouldn't cheat on me with another woman. I'm positive of that, so it doesn't bother me if other women look at him." She grinned and leaned closer to Luanne. "In fact, I kind of like it that other women think he's hot, too."

Luanne had narrowed her eyes and now sat studying Tess. "You really mean that?"

Tess laughed. "Come on, don't you like knowing you're with this gorgeous guy who only has eyes for you? It's a real thrill."

Luanne turned to Tyler. "You don't look at other women, do you?"

Rather than trying to sway her with a lot of flowery words, Tess knew the younger man was sincere when all he said was, "No."

"And even if women see you in these ads and throw themselves at you, you won't give in to temptation?" Luanne asked.

"Honey, women have been throwing themselves at me since my first rodeo, and I've never looked at a single one. Lots of the boys go crazy when they're out of town, but you know for a fact that I don't. Why would I start cheating now?"

He leaned over and placed a light kiss on his girlfriend's lips. "I love you, Luanne. I've loved you for years. If I do these ads, we'll have plenty of money to go ahead and get married now rather than waiting another year or so. Wouldn't you like to get married?"

Tears formed in Luanne's eyes. "Yes." She kissed Tyler long and hard, and Tess felt her throat tighten. The young couple was so obviously in love that it got to her. Automatically, her gaze went to Blake, who sat watching her intently.

She wished she knew what he was thinking, what he

was feeling. Did he care even a little bit about her or was it all fun and great sex to him? Did he suspect that she was crazy in love with him? More than likely. Blake was a smart man, and as Luanne had said, it was obvious to anyone who cared to look that she and Blake were involved.

It was probably equally obvious that she was in love with Blake.

"Okay. Whatever Tyler wants to do, I'll go along with," Luanne said when she ended the kiss. "I know he'd never do anything to hurt me. We've been dating for almost three years. He's a good man."

They kissed again, but broke off this time when a waiter appeared at the table. Thank goodness. Tess didn't relish spending the entire evening watching these two neck.

Knowing Luanne wasn't going to stand in the way of the ads made the tension seep out of Tess's body. Now that she no longer had that worry hanging over her head, she could relax and enjoy the evening.

Their time together turned out to be fun. They laughed and joked and had a great time. Repeatedly, her mind wandered to what would happen later once she and Blake returned to their hotel. She could hardly wait to be alone with him.

Finally, *finally*, after an almost two-hour dinner, she and Blake were back at the hotel. As soon as they entered his room, Tess wrapped herself around him, needing to be close to him. Needing to feel his touch. Desire hummed through her veins, and she met his mind-numbing kisses with her own.

"I thought we'd never get through that dinner," Blake said, tugging at her clothes. "I've been hungry for you since we were on the plane."

"Me, too." She nibbled on his bottom lip.

He captured her lips again, sliding his tongue inside her mouth. Tess groaned and held him closer.

When he finally lifted his head for air, he tugged at her dress. "Get naked, woman, or I won't be responsible for my actions."

Tess laughed and tugged on his shirt. "Hey, bucko, the same goes for you. I was the one who had to sit around listening to Luanne tell me how hot you are. You owe me a reward."

He raised one brow, pure devilment dancing in his eyes. "A reward? What sort of reward did you have in mind?"

"I haven't thought out all the details yet, but I know the first step is to get you naked."

Blake pulled his shirt out of his pants and slowly unbuttoned it. "Okay. I guess if I owe you, I owe you. I'm a man who always pays his debts."

"I'm counting on that," she said as she slid the zipper down on her dress. The passion in his eyes made her knees weak. "I'm definitely counting on that."

9

TESS STUDIED Blake's naked chest, desire making her heart pound. Slowly, she walked over and pushed his shirt from his shoulders.

"You know, I remember the day I came over to your apartment to tell you about the Desire Perfume account." She ran her hands across his skin, her fingers lingering in the matting of black hair. "I had a hard time talking to you because I was way too interested in your chest."

"Really? I would have never known." He grinned down at her. "Okay, maybe the way you kept staring at me did give you away a little. But other than that, I would have never known you were interested."

Rather than feeling self-conscious that he'd known she'd been lusting after him that day, she laughed softly. "Yes, your chest was a powerful distraction." After running her hands across that chest again, she skimmed down to his pants. "But your jeans were the real attention-getter."

Blake chuckled and kissed her temple. "Gee, want to tell me why?"

"Because they kept slipping lower. And lower. I was half expecting them to fall right off you."

Leaning back, his gaze met hers. "At that point in

our relationship, I'm pretty sure you would have run screaming from the room."

"Oh, no. Never." Tess studied him for a split second, debating how honest to be. Finally, she decided to go for broke. "I've lusted after you for quite some time."

He looked genuinely surprised. "I thought you didn't like me. In fact, you made your dislike known on several occasions."

"I didn't say I liked you. I said I lusted after you."

"Ah, well thanks for not sparing my feelings. So do you like me now?"

Tess wanted to tell him that she more than liked him, she loved him. But she knew their relationship couldn't take that kind of confidence. Blake would think she wanted a commitment out of him, when actually all she wanted was for him to be happy.

"Oh, I like you a lot now. But I also still lust after you. A lot. You're an incredibly handsome man, Blake. I'm no different than any other woman."

He cupped her face with his hands. "Yes, you are. You're different from any woman I've ever met."

Before she could answer, he kissed her slowly. Thoroughly. She slid her arms around his neck and kissed him back. When he finally lifted his head, desire burned in his eyes.

Blake fiddled with her dress until it dropped to her feet. Tess stepped out of it, kicking off her pumps at the same time.

"I lusted after you, too," he said.

Tess was stunned. She'd had no idea. He always

seemed to be making fun of her. "I thought you said I was a dried-up old prune."

"I like prunes," he teased. With ease, Blake flicked open the clasp on her bra and helped her take it off. "Besides, I knew a fire burned inside you. I knew making love with you would be phenomenal."

Tess leaned up on her tiptoes and kissed him again. She'd never kissed a man who tasted as wonderful as Blake. She could go on kissing him forever. "Before you, sex was kind of...awkward."

Blake slowly backed her toward the bed. When her knees hit the edge, Tess sat on the mattress. Blake stood in front of her, and Tess grinned. Tipping her head, she looked up at him. "Wait a minute, I have a fantasy about you that starts this way."

He'd been about to join her on the bed, but at her words, he stopped.

"Care to elaborate?" he asked, watching her closely.

With any other man, Tess wouldn't have had the courage to act out a fantasy. But this was Blake. She knew she could do whatever she wanted with him. To be absolutely certain, she asked, "You're certain you want to know about it?"

Blake grinned that sexy grin of his. "Sweetheart, feel free to do anything you want."

His soft, sensuous invitation was exactly what she wanted to hear. Tess drew a deep breath into her lungs, and then slowly slid his zipper down. Inch by inch, half expecting Blake to take over at any point. But he didn't. He stood still and let her explore.

When she slipped the fingers of one hand inside his

pants, he leaned down and whispered, "Looking for anything in particular?"

Tess gave him a flirty smile as she wrapped her fingers around his sizable erection. With long, lingering strokes, she caressed him. Blake made a soft, growling sound in his throat when she helped him take off his pants and his briefs. When he was naked, standing in front of her like the embodiment of every dream she'd ever had, she once again took his erection in her hands.

"Tess, you don't—"

She shushed him and kissed him intimately. "This is my fantasy. Not yours."

Blake's response as she took him into her mouth was a strangled moan and a husky, "You're wrong, sweetheart. This is definitely my fantasy, too."

That was the last thing either of them said for quite some time. Only later did Blake join Tess on the bed, pulling her into his arms. Feeling empowered by the intimacies they'd shared, she climbed on top of him, taking him into her body.

His hands cupped her breasts as she rode him, his gaze locked with hers. Tess knew a lot more was happening between them than just sex. She could see tenderness in his gaze, mixing with the burning-hot fire of passion. He might not be willing to admit even to himself that he cared for her, but Tess could read it clearly on his face.

"Tess," he groaned as he leaned up to kiss her.

She met him halfway, kissing him frantically as the tension grew within her. She knew he felt what was happening between them. Even though he wasn't interested in a lasting relationship, surely he could feel how magical they were together. Breaking the kiss, she moved with deliberate urgency, meeting his upward thrusts to bring them both to completion.

Afterward, she collapsed on top of him, happier than she could ever remember being in her life.

"Wow," she murmured, kissing his chest. "You're truly an amazing man, Blake Sutherland."

She felt soft laughter rumble through him. "Glad you can remember my name because I sure can't."

BLAKE LIGHTLY STROKED Tess's hair as he felt his heart rate slow to normal. Tess thought he was amazing. Why? Because he could make her howl with pleasure?

He felt unsettled by what they'd just shared. Sure, the sex had redefined the word amazing. But for him, sex had never felt so consuming before. So powerful. In the past, sex had been about having a good time, pleasing himself and the woman he was with.

But as Tess had loved him both times tonight, he'd once again felt more than simple physical pleasure. So much more. He felt as if she was finding all the dark, lonely places in his soul and filling them with light. Every time he was with Tess, he knew a lot more was happening than mere sex.

Part of the difference was because Tess loved him. He could see love in her eyes when she looked at him. Okay, maybe not all the time. Every once in a while she still liked to give him those schoolmarm frowns she specialized in. But most of the time, her love for him flashed like a neon sign. His mother had seen it. Luanne had seen it. They'd seen love on Tess's face.

Which left him with one hell of a problem. What kind of bastard would he be if he kept having sex with Tess knowing she was in love with him? She was going to get hurt when things ended. And they would end. His relationships always did.

But thinking about not seeing Tess made a dull ache grow in his chest. He might not be in love, but he cared for her. Tess was sweet and fun, but she also pushed him to be the best person he could be. Since he did care for her, he needed to make certain she would be okay when their time together ended.

Blake shifted so Tess rested next to him, then curved her body against his. "Honey, about us—"

"Oh no. This sounds like a do-you-know-what-you're-doing-young-lady talk to me. I hope not, because I'm having one heck of a time fooling around with you, Blake. Don't get all serious on me, okay?"

He didn't buy her flippant tone for a second. Tess could pretend all she wanted that she didn't love him, but he knew better. One thing the last few weeks had taught him was how to read her. He knew he was right about her feelings.

Just as he knew she was going to get hurt. He had to try again. "I don't want you to end up—"

Again, she interrupted him, this time by placing her fingers over his lips. "Don't. Don't do this, Blake. Can't we just be together, at least until the Loverboy account is finished? Then, after that, we can sit down and have a long talk. But until then, can't we simply enjoy ourselves? I've never experienced what I'm experiencing with you. I can't imagine living out my fantasies with any other man. Is it wrong that I want what we're sharing to last a little while longer?"

Blake leaned over her, kissing her gently. No, what she was asking wasn't wrong. Still, he couldn't help feeling selfish, because a better man would walk away. A better man wouldn't break her heart.

But he wasn't that man. Whether it was the right thing to do or not, he was going to take her up on her offer.

"Yes," he said as he ended the kiss.

Rather than being solemn and stern, Tess grinned at him as if he'd given her snow on Christmas morning. "Yes? That's all you can say? You're this hotshot, creative guy and 'yes' is the best answer you can come up with when I say I want to explore my fantasies with you? Seems kind of puny."

Blake laughed and settled his body over hers. "How about yahoo? Or yippee?"

Tess rolled her eyes, making Blake laugh even harder. When he cupped a soft breast in one hand, inspiration struck him.

"I know, how about hot damn?"

This time, Tess was the one to laugh. "That's more like it. I like to see enthusiasm."

"We aim to please, ma'am," Blake said a fraction of a second before he kissed her breast. "We aim to please."

TESS LEANED OVER her desk and studied the photographs of the latest Loverboy model, Will LaFontaine.

The young man certainly was photogenic. Perfect for the campaign.

She still couldn't believe how easy the trip to New Orleans had been. After they'd checked into their hotel, a bellhop had ridden up in the elevator with them. On the way, he and Blake had chatted about the broiling weather. Then, the young man had mentioned he volunteered at a senior citizen center where many of the folks could remember even worse summers than this one.

Blake had looked at Tess. Tess had looked at Blake. She'd shifted the luggage cart aside and really looked at the young man. Handsome. He was definitely handsome.

Within minutes, they'd outlined the Loverboy campaign. Then, after Will got off work, they'd met him at the senior center and learned he'd been volunteering there for years.

Too perfect.

Debra had been thrilled with the latest Loverboy, especially since Blake and Tess had found him so quickly. She'd been doubly thrilled when the first billboards featuring Tyler had gone up in cities around the country and print ads had appeared in national magazines.

Things were going exceptionally well, which made Tess nervous. In her experience whenever life seemed to be going smoothly, it was only a matter of time before something bad happened.

But maybe this time she was only sensing the day

when she and Blake would have to break things off between them. He knew she loved him, that much was clear. And he was worried about her getting hurt, which only made her love him more. With each passing day, she sensed him getting more and more anxious about their relationship. Blake was a nice guy, and he didn't want to take advantage of her.

Tess was the one who wanted to take advantage of him. All of her life, she'd been the rule follower. She never disappeared for weeks at a time. She always balanced her checkbook and worried about the feelings of others. She never did a single thing even remotely wild or daring.

Blake was her wild time. Sure, it wouldn't last. And sure, she'd be hurt when it ended. But in the meantime, she would enjoy every second and explore a few of her fantasies along the way. Then, when they broke up, she'd have a lot of really terrific memories tucked away for the future.

And more importantly, her relationship with Blake was making her a stronger person. She felt free and adventurous around him. No longer would she be content to settle for second best. Thanks to Blake, she knew she was a vital, sexy woman who deserved everything life had to offer.

Grabbing a few of the headshots of Will off her desk, Tess headed toward Blake's office. She'd just knocked on the doorjamb when she realized Blake wasn't alone. A young, dark-haired woman sat in one of the chairs facing his desk.

"Oops. Sorry," Tess said, taking a step back.

"Come on in." Blake stood and waved Tess inside. "This is my sister, Lisa."

Tess walked over and shook Lisa's hand. This close, she could easily see the resemblance between the siblings. Like her brother, Lisa had pitch-black hair and blue eyes.

"Hi, Tess. I've heard all about you." Lisa grinned as she looked at her brother. "Mom still can't believe you're willing to put up with Blake. She said you were such a nice woman she would have expected you to toss Blake out by now."

"Hey," Blake said with a mock frown. "Is that any way to talk to your brother?"

Lisa's grin only grew wider. "Especially a brother who pays all the bills? Um, let me rethink this." She looked back at Tess. "You are so fortunate to work with such a paragon. Blake is an absolute angel. A creative genius who could find a job anywhere."

"He is creative," Tess murmured, flashing a quick glance at Blake. "Very creative."

"You betcha," Lisa said. "In fact, he was so popular at his old job that Jeff Markland, the president of the company where Blake used to work, tried several times to talk him out of leaving. So consider yourself lucky. He could be making megabucks if he'd stayed at Markland and Jacobs. And I might mention, that's money I could use for a car."

Laughing, Lisa turned back to her brother. "How'd I do? Think she's impressed with you yet?"

Blake shook his head. "There is no way I can be related to you. Mom must be lying to us."

Tess smiled, enjoying the repartee between Blake and his sister, but even as the two joked, she couldn't help feeling disconcerted by what Lisa had said. Blake had left a high-paying job to come work at D&S Advertising. If he helped both his mother and his sister out financially, working here must leave him pretty strapped.

When the siblings started discussing whether or not Lisa truly needed a car, Tess excused herself and headed back to her own office. On the way, she swung by Molly's desk to see how she was doing. With only three more weeks until the baby was due to arrive, their receptionist was moving very slowly these days.

"Hi. How's junior holding out today?" Tess asked.

Molly rubbed her back. "He's making touchdowns inside me."

Pulling out the chair next to Molly's desk, Tess sat. "I think it's about time you consider staying home. I know you said you only wanted to take off six weeks after the baby arrived, but that may not be enough."

Molly nodded. "I know. I'm starting to think the same thing myself. I have a doctor's appointment today. Let me see what she says."

Since this was so important to Tess, she offered, "If it's about your salary, Blake and I talked on our trip to New Orleans. We'll give you an additional two weeks of paid maternity leave."

"That's great," Molly said, beaming. "I can't tell you how much I appreciate it." She stood and came over to hug Tess, not an easy task since she was so far along in her pregnancy. "You and Blake have been terrific, first by buying the baby's crib, now by giving me all this time off."

"It's our pleasure," Tess said, meaning it. When Molly sat back down, Tess noticed she had tears forming in her eyes. "Our concern is for your well-being. We want to make certain you and the baby are fine."

Molly grabbed Tess's hand and pressed it against the top of her swollen abdomen. "Feel him kick. That's one healthy boy."

Tess suppressed a smile. Ever since the baby had started to move, Molly had been getting people to feel his kicks. At first, Tess had been reluctant to touch the other woman's stomach. But now she was comfortable feeling the baby.

Except this time when the little boy kicked against her hand, Tess felt something more. Something deeper. A joy mingled with sadness. While she was thrilled for Molly and her husband, Tess suddenly realized how very much she wanted to be a mom. She wanted to feel new life growing inside her. She wanted to feel so loved by a man that she'd long for his child.

Shocked by the intensity of her feelings, Tess pulled her hand away from Molly's stomach.

"He's quite athletic," she told the younger woman. Standing, she added, "Be sure to let me know what the doctor says this afternoon."

"Will do," Molly assured Tess.

After that, Tess headed back to her office and closed the door behind her. Normally, she left her office door open, but right now, she needed some quiet time to think. According to Lisa, Blake's prior boss had asked him several times to reconsider leaving. Knowing how much money he used to make and how sorry they were to see him leave, Tess couldn't help wondering how Jason had convinced him to join D&S Advertising.

She felt even worse knowing that Blake had left such a lucrative job only to end up holding down the fort with her. But what bothered her most about what Lisa had said was knowing that Blake obviously shouldered the financial responsibility for both his mother and his sister. He earned the same salary she did, which wasn't much at the moment. And probably anything he'd saved from his other job had been invested in D&S Advertising.

Working here had to be very difficult for him.

D&S needed to grow a lot bigger before Blake could earn more money. Truthfully, if they did get a loan or find an investor, they needed to use the money to expand and form a more competitive company. One that could go after the truly big clients.

But if she left D&S and pulled out her money, the company's future would be precarious. How could she leave Blake with that sort of mess? Plus, after all they'd managed to accomplish during the past few weeks, she didn't want to walk away from D&S Advertising. She enjoyed the thrill of coming up with new ideas and seeing them put into action.

Granted, she was a novice at this business, but she was having a great time. She knew a large part of the reason why she enjoyed the work was because she was with Blake, but that wasn't the only reason. She liked being part of something creative.

The question became, if she didn't let Blake buy her out, could she continue to work with him after their personal relationship ended? What would it be like to see him day after day and no longer be free to touch him or kiss him? To no longer laugh and smile and lust when he came into her office to torment her with all the wonderful things he planned on doing to her later when they were alone?

And what would happen when he got involved with someone else? Could she really plaster a smile on her face and be nice to some other woman who was sleeping with Blake?

Not in this lifetime.

A firm tap on her door had Tess sitting up straight in her chair. "Come in."

Blake came inside, shutting the door behind him. "Hey. What's up? You feeling okay?"

He came over to her side of the desk. Tess couldn't decide how honest she should be with him. Would he understand if she told him she wanted to stay with D&S Advertising but couldn't stand the thought of working with him once they were no longer lovers?

Or should she admit that it worried her that he took care of so many people?

Instead, she stood and kissed him, pouring all of her love into the embrace.

When the kiss finally ended, Blake gave her a sexy little smile. "Wow. What did I do to deserve that?"

She gently caressed one side of his face. He was so handsome, and she loved it when he looked at her the way he was now. As if she were the only woman in the world. The only woman he desired.

"I really admire you," she said softly, still touching his face. "You're such a sweet man."

Blake stilled her hands by covering them with his own. "You think I'm sweet?"

"Yes. Very much."

His easy grin made her heart race. "Really? Then my plan is working. I've lured you into thinking I'm this great guy. That will make it oh-so-much easier to have my wicked way with you."

The sadness that had settled over her evaporated under the warmth of his teasing.

"Hey, I said you were sweet. I didn't say a thing about letting you have your way with me, wicked or not."

Blake fiddled with the top button of her silk blouse. "Sure you will. I know all the places you like to be touched. Ten minutes flat, and you'll be putty in my hands."

"Ten minutes? More like five." She was already hungry for his touch. For his kisses. "I don't have time to let you prove your point right now, but I'm willing to let you try your best later tonight," she said.

"You're on."

She leaned up to kiss him again, but he stopped her.

"Are you okay?" he asked.

His serious tone surprised her. "Sure. Why do you ask?"

He dropped a kiss on her nose. "You seemed a little

sad when I came in. Any problems I should know about? Maybe I can help."

He should know what she was thinking. The future of D&S affected both of them. Moving out of his embrace, she sat back down in her chair. Blake perched on the edge of her desk.

"What's up?"

Collecting her thoughts, Tess said slowly, "I've been thinking about what happens to D&S after we secure additional financing. The business really needs to expand. If I take my money out of the company, then you won't be able to grow the business the way you need to if you want to go after bigger clients. Advertising is competitive. You'll need to exploit the momentum you'll gain from the Desire Perfume account. If you buy me out, you won't have any money left."

Blake's gaze never wavered from hers. She wished she could tell what he was thinking, but his expression gave nothing away. "Are you saying you want to stay with D&S?"

Tess sighed. "To tell you the truth, I don't know what I want, Blake. All I know is I want to make certain the company will be okay. I want to know you'll be fine."

"You know I'll be fine," he said.

"But will you be able to draw a big enough salary to fulfill your obligations?"

Blake nodded. "Ah, I see. This is about Lisa, right?" He leaned toward her. "I appreciate your concern, sweetheart, but I'm fine. Lisa's situation isn't a problem."

Tess didn't believe him for a second. He was only saying that so she wouldn't worry. How had she ever thought this man was anything like her irresponsible brother and father? Blake Sutherland was anything but irresponsible. He might not be interested in love and marriage, but he also was the kind of man who wouldn't let a woman down. He'd always been honest with her, and she knew when their relationship ended he'd be as considerate as possible of her feelings.

Tess chose a different approach. "But what about the company? What about the employees? How will you make payroll if you buy me out?"

"I'll make sure I get enough capital to buy you out and also grow the company. I won't let the employees down." He narrowed his eyes and studied her. "What's really going on, Tess? What brought all this up now?"

"I was talking to Molly, and I told her that you and I decided to give her additional maternity leave."

"And you were worried she might not have a job to come back to if she took off eight weeks, right?"

She nodded. "Yes. She deserves to have her job waiting for her when her leave is up."

"It will be," Blake assured her. "But you know I can't help thinking there's more on your mind than whether Molly's job will still be waiting for her. Are you reluctant to have me buy you out because you want to stay?"

His perceptiveness caught her off guard, and she saw no reason not to be up-front with him. "I've enjoyed working on the Loverboy account. It's been a lot of fun."

Blake chuckled. "Which part? Coming up with the idea? Finding the models? Or making wild, crazy love with your business partner?"

"I've enjoyed all of it."

He raised one eyebrow. "Equally?"

"There have been one or two things I've enjoyed more than the others," she admitted.

Blake had just leaned down to kiss her when the phone rang.

"Remind me later tonight to find out what those things are," he said, releasing her and heading for the door. Right before he walked out, he added, "And don't worry about the company. It will be fine, Tess, and I'll be fine."

But as she reached for her phone, she couldn't help wondering if she would be fine.

10

BLAKE SLIPPED on his sunglasses and stared out at the Atlantic Ocean. Miami was hot, but they caught a nice breeze being this close to the water. They'd spent most of yesterday and today looking for Loverboy candidates. Unlike New Orleans, and later Cleveland, no one had dropped into their laps. This time, they'd had to work to find someone. Finally luck had turned their way when, just after lunch, they'd found a young man, Herve Quintero, who mentored underprivileged youths.

"I can't think of a better place to end the Loverboy campaign than here," Tess admitted with a sigh as she looked at the ocean. "It's heaven. Like a travel poster."

Blake reached for her hand. As he wrapped his fingers around hers, he wondered how long it would be before one of them brought up the obvious—today, they'd pretty much finished the Loverboy account. Sure, a few photo shoots and details remained, but they'd found all six candidates.

So did that mean they ended their affair now or did they wait a bit longer?

His cell phone rang, and Blake grabbed it. Without even looking at the number, he had a pretty good idea who it was. Jeff Markland, his old boss at Markland

and Jacobs. Jeff had called him three times in the last week, always wanting the same thing—to have Blake return to the fold.

Blake shot a look at Tess, who seemed absorbed in the scenery. But he knew better. Tess didn't miss a thing. Even only hearing his side of the conversation, she'd know what the call was about. He considered moving inside the hotel, but decided against it. He needed to be honest with Tess.

Jeff wasted no time after Blake answered the phone. He launched right into all the reasons he thought Blake should return to Markland and Jacobs.

When the other man finally took a breath, Blake said, "Jeff, I appreciate it, but I don't think—"

"Hang on a sec, Blake. I'm not through. We loved what you did with Neat and Tidy Cleaner. And the new Loverboy campaign is terrific."

"The idea for Loverboy was my business partner's, Tess Denison."

At her name, Tess turned and looked questioningly at him. When they'd gotten back from the interview with Herve, she'd changed into a sexy, flowered sundress. He wanted to skim that dress off her and spend the rest of the afternoon and tonight in bed.

But that wouldn't be fair. Not while there were so many unanswered questions between them. He met her gaze, but continued to listen to Jeff. After a moment, she stood and wandered across the outdoor restaurant to look in the window of a small beach shop.

"Stan and I were wrong to let you leave Markland

and Jacobs," Jeff said. "You have vision and a heck of a way with people."

"Thanks, I appreciate that. But I'm happy."

Jeff laughed, "Oh, not you. I know you're not happy unless you're getting ahead. And I've got just the offer for you."

"Honestly, Jeff, I can't—"

"We want you to be a partner. We're willing to give you options, a signing bonus, the whole nine yards."

Blake was stunned, but didn't say anything as his old boss outlined the lucrative package they'd put together for him. With that kind of money, his financial worries about his mother and sister would disappear. Plus, Jeff was offering him creative freedom at the agency. Blake would have the chance to do what he loved to do while having the safety net of a strong client base. It was exactly what he wanted, what he'd always wanted. And he didn't owe anything to Jason. His friend had already bailed on the company.

But he owed Tess.

Almost as if she knew he was thinking about her, Tess glanced at him. Yeah, he owed her all right. He owed her for sticking with D&S after Jason left.

On a personal level, he owed it to her to get out of her life before he messed it up any more than he already had. He'd been selfish to let things go on as long as they had.

"So, what do you say?" Jeff asked. "You on board? We'd like you back ASAP, but we realize you have to tie up loose ends there."

As he watched, Tess headed back toward the table.

When she got close, she slowly smiled at him, a hesitant is-everything-all-right smile. As much as he wanted to, he didn't smile back.

He couldn't.

"Jeff, I'm really interested, but I need a couple of days to think about it. I'll call you the first of next week."

Jeff sighed. "Not the answer I wanted, but I'll settle for it. And see if you can think it over quickly. Markland and Jacobs wants you back soon."

"I'll call," Blake promised as he hung up.

"Problem?" Tess asked as she sat down.

"I guess you figured out who that was."

Tess stirred her iced tea, her gaze on her glass. "Jeff Markland, right? The man you used to work for."

"He wants me to come back," Blake admitted. He reached across the table to take her hand in his, but before he could, she settled both of her hands in her lap.

"I thought you wanted to be your own boss," she said.

Blake felt like someone was squeezing his heart. "I do. But Jeff and Stan are offering me the chance to be a partner."

Tess's mouth flattened into a straight line. "I see. Sounds perfect for you."

"Tess, I didn't say yes." He wasn't certain why he told her that since he didn't want to give her false hope. But she looked so resigned, almost as if she'd expected him to bail on her.

Then it hit him. She had. After the way her father and Jason acted, she probably figured it was only a matter of time before he walked. And here he was, about to prove her right.

At this moment, Blake hated himself.

"You're going to say yes." Tess met his gaze. "Aren't you?"

"Probably," he admitted. "But you already want out of D&S, and Jason doesn't look like he's ever coming back. With the money from the Loverboy account, you can recoup your original investment. Hell, even Jason can get his money back. Markland and Jacobs are offering me enough of a hiring bonus to more than replace the money I put into D&S. So then everyone will be happy."

Except Tess didn't look even remotely happy, although he knew she was trying. She gave him a small smile and said, "I understand what you're saying, and I also understand why you want to go back to Markland and Jacobs. You can do what you want and earn a great salary. I know that's important to you, especially since you help out your mom and sister."

Blake sighed. Damn. Why did this have to be so difficult? He didn't want to hurt Tess; he cared about her deeply. Probably too deeply. But things were building too slowly at D&S to solve his financial obligations anytime soon. That meant he had to go after a loan or an investor, which meant rules and restrictions. In his experience, people didn't invest in a company without wanting a say in how the company was run.

He leaned forward, wanting her to know how much this decision hurt him. "I've checked, Tess. Every bank or investment group wants to have a strong say in how

D&S operates. It won't be like having our own business. It will be like working for someone else. Truthfully, I'll have more autonomy at Markland and Jacobs."

Tess nodded slowly, but he had no idea what she was thinking. Did she hate him? Probably.

"I'm not leaving you, Tess," he said. "I'm not like your father or Jason. You already want out of the company. What do you care if I leave as well?"

Tess gave him a sad smile. "The funny thing is I plan on staying."

"So, you've definitely decided?"

"Well, yes. It may be bumpy in the beginning, but I think I'll at least try." She ran her thumb down the side of her iced tea glass, the motion making a path in the condensation. When she looked back at him, there was a sheen of moisture in her eyes. "I've enjoyed working with you. I think we're good together."

"We are good together, Tess. But I have obligations. Responsibilities. Jeff Markland is offering me a huge salary and a partnership." He felt like a total jerk leaving her this way, but what else could he do? Stay with D&S and tell his sister she had to drop out of grad school?

"It's a wonderful opportunity," Tess said.

Blake ran his hands through his hair. "Tess, let's say you stay with D&S and we go after capital, is that the kind of company you want to work for? One where we have to answer to other people?"

She shook her head. "No. Look, I realize it will take

some time for us to grow the business, but I can't help thinking—"

He hated to ask, but he had to. "Is this about us? Our relationship? Do you think if we both stayed with D&S, we could continue to be lovers?"

Tess's gaze locked with his own. He felt his chest squeeze tight when she said, "I'm realistic about our relationship, Blake. I know it has to end."

"Now?"

Even as he said the word, a sharp sensation hit him, followed immediately by the realization that he loved Tess. He'd loved her for a long time, but now he knew it deep within his soul. He truly loved her.

But loving her didn't change a thing. If anything it made it more imperative to end their affair, before he hurt her too deeply. Tess deserved better than he could give her. He needed to establish his career, and the job at Markland and Jacobs would take up all of his time for at least a few years. He couldn't be there for her the way she deserved.

"How soon will you start your new job?" she asked.

"I haven't said yes," he repeated.

"You're going to. So how soon do you start?" Her gaze was clear, resigned. He hated to think how many times she'd dealt with disappointment in the past. Tess seemed like a pro at being let down.

"I won't leave until we finish the Loverboy account. There's still a lot of work to be done."

"Not much. A week or two."

A waiter stopped by their table, but Blake waved

him away. "I don't want to do this, Tess, but we knew from the beginning we weren't going to last."

"True. And I'm okay with it ending, Blake. I know you don't believe me, but I am."

She was right. He didn't believe her. Hell, he wasn't okay with their breakup, but it was the only reasonable thing to do.

For a couple of minutes, she simply gazed out at the Atlantic Ocean. Then she tipped her head and looked at him.

"I have a request. Since this is the end of our affair, then I think we should make the most of tonight," she said, all trace of sadness gone from her face. "We should end this affair like adults. Be civilized. Let's have a nice dinner, make love. Once." She smiled. "Or more times. Tomorrow we head back to Chicago. When we get back there, we can officially end our relationship. We'll also make plans for you to start your new job."

Startled, Blake looked at her. She couldn't be serious. "You're kidding, right?"

"Not at all. Why shouldn't we end this affair as well as we started it?"

Frankly, he was speechless, for a moment at least. When he recovered, the best he could come up with was, "Because no one breaks up this nicely."

Tess laughed softly, seemingly content with the way things were. "Then they should. Who says you have to have a huge fight when you break up? I told you all along that I knew our personal relationship wouldn't last forever. You knew that, too."

"Well, sure, but—"

She leaned toward him. "Are you angry that you had an affair with me?"

"No, of course not."

"And we both agree now is the right time to end our affair, right?"

Damn, she was making this sound so reasonable, but it wasn't at all. Who broke up like this? She couldn't be serious.

"Tess, pretending you're not upset isn't going to help."

"I know what I want. I've known all along what I want. I like being with you, and I really enjoy making love with you. But you and I were never meant to last. You knew it. I knew it. Let's spare each other the tears, have a really great time tonight, and tomorrow, we'll head back home. Now, what's wrong with that?"

He was certain if he took a minute, he could think of a reason or two. Unfortunately, nothing popped into his head quickly enough.

"Nothing's wrong with it, I guess. It just seems strange."

Tess finished her iced tea and smiled sweetly at him. "I don't think it's strange at all. But if you prefer, I'll burst into tears and run to my room. Will that make you feel better?"

Despite himself, he smiled. "Of course not. I never wanted to make you unhappy."

"Good. Then let's get this show on the road." She glanced at her watch. "Why don't we go for a swim now, then maybe we can make love before dinner. I think, since we don't have a lot of time before our plane leaves tomorrow, we can have dinner in the hotel." The look she gave him was sexy and sassy. "Or maybe room service, instead."

"Um, Tess—"

"Still, it would be romantic to have dinner in the dining room, then go dancing in the lounge afterward. After that, we can go back to the room and make love again. What do you think?"

What did he think? He thought she was crazy. But hey, if she wanted to schedule their last night together, who was he to disagree? Even though she didn't look the part at the moment, Tess was in serious schoolmarm mode.

"Why don't we see how the evening progresses, okay?" he asked.

This time when Tess smiled at him, she seemed way too happy for his peace of mind. Sure, he didn't want her to be miserable, but he also hadn't expected her to be so damn accepting of the situation. A few tears might have been a nice touch. Instead, she was organizing the end of their affair.

Too bad he didn't feel at all enthusiastic about this. But whether she was serious or just pretending about tonight, he was going to do his damnedest to make certain she had a wonderful time. Then, when she thought about him years from now, maybe she'd have a few happy memories. Maybe she'd even look back on their affair and smile, remembering how much fun they'd had.

Maybe she wouldn't hate him. But he sure wouldn't count on it.

"DID YOU PACK EVERYTHING?" Tess asked as she walked into Blake's office two weeks later. The room was barren, just like she knew it would be. Looking around, she felt unbelievably sad. Blake was really leaving.

With effort, she made herself smile. "Looks like you got it all."

Blake leaned against his desk, now devoid of any personal items. "Yeah. I got everything."

"Good. Wouldn't want you to leave anything behind." Tess forced herself to sound cheerful, but she knew Blake didn't believe her routine.

"I'm sorry things ended this way," he said.

When he made a move to come over to her, she took a couple of steps back. She didn't want him to touch her. If he did, she was certain she would cry.

"Things worked out the way they were meant to work out," she told him. "The only way they could've worked out. We had a great time." She took a deep breath and added, "I'll always remember you."

Blake took a couple of steps toward her. "Tess, tell me you're okay."

"The company will be fine. I'll be fine." When he frowned, she changed it to "I am fine."

"I wish I believed that."

She looked at him, her heart in her throat. This conversation was more difficult than she'd expected. For the last couple of weeks since they'd returned from Miami, they'd been tense around each other. Really tense. Although they'd both made an effort to smooth the tension, nothing had worked. Every day had been a torment, seeing him, discussing the business with him, but no longer able to touch him. To be with him.

And now Blake was leaving. Tess could only hope that once he was gone, she could finally start piecing together her broken heart.

"I appreciate everything you did for D&S," she said, hoping to move the conversation to a less personal level. "The Loverboy ads turned out great. And even with Molly on maternity leave, the office is running like a well-oiled machine."

"Is there anything else I can do for you?" he asked.

Oh, now there was a leading question. Tess could think of a million things he could do that would make her happy. But she didn't say a word. She merely shook her head.

"What will you do if Jason doesn't return?"

"He will. Soon he'll be back charming the clients like nothing ever happened. Like he never disappeared in the first place. But even if he doesn't come back, I'll be fine." She gave Blake a faint smile, her throat tightening, her eyes stinging with tears she refused to shed. "I'll be okay, and finding financing shouldn't be that difficult. Once I have the funds, I'll send you a check for your original investment."

"I've told you a dozen times, you don't need to repay me."

She held his gaze. This point was non-negotiable. She was going to buy him out. "Yes. I do."

Blake must have considered the wisdom of starting the same fight all over again on his last day here because he didn't argue. He merely shrugged. "Whatever you want."

"I want to buy you out. And I will. It just may take a little while."

"I'm in no hurry."

Thank goodness, since Tess knew it would indeed take her some time before she could send him the money. But she would do it.

"I appreciate your understanding," she said, hating how stiff and distant they sounded around each other. It was hard to believe that only a couple of weeks ago in Miami, they'd been lovers. Now they seemed like strangers.

"You're an extraordinary woman," he said softly.

His compliment almost made her cry. "Thank you, Blake. Have a nice life."

"You, too."

Then before she did anything to embarrass herself, she gave him one last long look and walked out.

BLAKE SURVEYED the stack of mail on his desk at Markland and Jacobs and realized he hated his job. Gut-level hated it, which was stupid. This job was everything he'd wanted for years. The only problem was now that he had it, he hated it. The last month had been torture.

Talk about irony. This was all Tess's fault. She'd made him hate this job. By being fun. By being smart. By being sexy. He missed her so much he thought he'd go crazy sometimes. He couldn't help wondering if she missed him, too. Even a little bit.

Probably not. Her life was full now. She had the agency. Jason might even be back.

He glanced at the perfect clock on his perfect desk, figuring this day had to be over by now. He felt as if he'd been here for days. But rather than showing 5:00 p.m., the clock showed 11:00 a.m., which couldn't be right.

Frustration gnawed at him, so he decided to take an early lunch. Maybe go for a ride and clear his head. Figure out why, when he'd finally gotten everything he wanted in life, he was abjectly miserable.

But as soon as he left the office, he didn't head toward his favorite restaurant. He didn't even head for a scenic drive. He headed toward his mother's house.

"What's wrong?" Kathleen asked the second she saw him on her front porch.

"Jeez, can't a guy stop by for lunch without there being something wrong?"

Kathleen hustled him into her small kitchen. "A normal guy can. A workaholic like you can't. So, what's wrong?"

Blake chuckled and walked over to the refrigerator. He'd stocked it this past weekend, so he knew there was plenty to eat. Grabbing a selection of cold cuts, lettuce and mustard, he asked, "How about a sandwich?"

Kathleen tried to take the food away from him, but he pointed at the table.

"Sit. I'm fixing lunch."

But he questioned the wisdom of his pronouncement when he realized Kathleen now had nothing to do but think up a never-ending list of questions for him. What was wrong? How was his job? Why did he look so tired? Blake quickly realized she wasn't going to stop until he addressed why he was here.

"I'm feeling restless at work, that's all," he assured her. "No big deal."

"That's where you're wrong. No offense, but I thought I'd raised a smart son."

Blake glanced at her over his shoulder. "Hey. Watch the insults."

"You know what I mean. You hate that job. It's plain as day. You hate it because you loved being at D&S."

Blake finished making two ham sandwiches and set them on the table. After pouring two glasses of iced tea, he settled across the table from his mother.

"D&S was fun, Mom, but I'm making about four times as much money now." Realizing how that sounded, he quickly added, "Plus, with Jason gone, there wasn't much point in sticking around. I only joined because of him."

His mother frowned at him. "Pooh. I don't believe a thing you're saying, and neither do you. You may have joined because of Jason, but you liked working there because of Tess."

"Yeah, Tess was fun." He bit into his sandwich, hoping his mother would drop the subject.

Naturally she didn't. "So tell me, did you leave because Markland and Jacobs offered you so much money or because your love affair with Tess ended badly?"

Blake almost choked. "Mom, I left because of the money."

She nodded slowly. "I see. So then what happened between you and Tess? Did you break up or are you still seeing each other?"

"We were friends. And partners."

"And lovers," his mother said emphatically. "I'm not blind. I know you two were a couple. I could see how much she loved you on her face."

Blake realized there was no point in pretending with his mother. She was just too sharp. He set the remainder of his sandwich on his plate and looked at her. "I worry about Tess."

"Call her. Tell her you love her, too."

Blake shook his head. "No, I don't."

His mother made a very unladylike snorting noise. "Of course you do. I can see it quite clearly as well. You love her. You're fooling yourself if you don't think so."

"Even if we did get back together, how long will it last? Another month? A year?" He gave her a sharp look. "Then Tess and I will be right back where we are now."

"How can you say that? A lot of people manage to make love last."

"Name me one couple," Blake scoffed.

His mother sighed. "Okay, I know your life wasn't perfect. You had to help out way too much after your dad died. But to this day, I miss him. Don't get me wrong, marriage is hard work. But nobody is a harder worker than you are. Things could really work for you and Tess."

"And if it doesn't? I end up making Tess miserable."

His mother smiled. "I can guarantee you she's already miserable. You have to try to make her happy. This is your shot at happiness, Blake. Don't blow it because you're a coward."

A coward? Was he really a coward? Maybe he was. What if his mother was right, and this was his shot at happiness? Could he really walk away from Tess?

He knew he couldn't. He owed it to himself, and to Tess, to at least try for the happy ending.

With his mind made up, he looked at his mother. "I need to at least tell her how I feel."

"Exactly. All you have to do is go see Tess, tell her you love her, and you'll live happily ever after."

"It's not that simple. What if she won't believe me? Besides, for all I know, she may be involved with someone else by now."

"Nonsense. She loves you. I'm positive of that. But if you want to help convince her to take you back, then do something big. Something so wonderful she can't help knowing how much you love her. Be amazing. We women like that in a man."

The tightness in his chest suddenly eased, replaced by a feeling of expectation. His mother was right. He could do this. He could really have it all.

Except...

"I can ask Tess to marry me, but I can't leave Markland and Jacobs. D&S doesn't make a lot right now."

His mother leaned back in her chair and grabbed the

phone off the kitchen wall. "I'm calling Lisa to come over here. We need to sort out a few things. If you left D&S so you can make enough money to support Lisa and me, then we're going to change that."

Putting his hand over hers, he said, "You're assuming too much, Mom. First, I like helping you and Lisa. You're my family. I love you."

"I know. But I'm not letting you stay at a job you hate because of me. And neither is Lisa. I'm calling her over here, and we're going to figure out how to reduce how much we cost you. That way, you can go back to D&S."

After calling his sister and telling her to hustle over to the house, Kathleen smiled broadly, happiness twinkling in her blue eyes. "This is wonderful. Absolutely wonderful. I'm going to have a daughter-in-law."

"Hey. Aren't you getting ahead of yourself? Tess may tell me to take a hike. You forget, men tend to take off on her. Her father. Her brother. They leave all the time. I left her, too."

Kathleen leaned toward him, her expression intense but full of love. "I may not know a lot of things, but I know this. You left Tess and D&S for Lisa and me. That's a responsible man. Tess knows that. She knows you're not like the men in her family. You're a good person, Blake. Maybe too good sometimes." She patted his hand. "Don't worry. Lisa and I will help you convince Tess to marry you. She might be able to say no to one Sutherland, but she won't be able to resist three."

Blake smiled, feeling better for the first time since

he'd been in Miami with Tess. Maybe his mother was right. Maybe he could convince Tess to marry him.

Resisting three Sutherlands would be almost impossible.

11

"WHAT DO YOU MEAN Blake no longer works there?" Jason said on the phone. "Tess, I leave for a few days and everything falls apart. What happened? Did you have a big fight with him? I thought you two were getting along. I mean, come on, you were sleeping with him. That's something else we need to talk about."

Tess shifted the receiver to her other ear. Since Blake had left, she'd spent most of her time trying to forget him. But forgetting Blake was proving difficult. Make that impossible. No matter what she was doing, no matter how hard she tried, she couldn't stop thinking about him.

And missing him. Oh, how she missed him.

"I didn't drive Blake away and, for the record, you've been gone for months, not days. You have no right commenting on how I've run this business. You haven't been here."

"Look, Tessie, I wasn't trying to—"

Tess drew in a deep breath and decided she'd had enough. "Jason, you and I have to talk. If we're going to continue being partners, you can't simply walk away whenever the craving grabs you. You're either in or out. At this point, I consider you out."

"Drawing a line in the sand for me?" Jason's voice contained a hint of humor.

He didn't believe her. Didn't believe his sweet sister would stand up to him. Boy, was he in for a surprise. She'd learned a lot over the last few weeks. As long as she let her brother take advantage of her, he would. She had to stop him.

"Here's the deal," she said. "We're going to have a partners' contract that stipulates if you ever walk away again, I get your shares in the business."

"I won't sign that."

"Then I'll sell the shares Blake and I own in the company to investors. They won't let you simply wander off. It's your choice. If you want this business, you have to promise not to desert it again. This isn't a game, Jason. You're either part of this, or you're not."

She could practically hear Jason debating her ultimatum. Frankly, she didn't care what he decided. If he stayed with the company, he needed to be a true partner. If he decided to walk, well, she'd find other investors and keep the company afloat that way. Either way, it felt wonderful to stand up for herself.

All traces of humor were gone from his voice when he finally said, "Since you've left me no choice, I guess I'll sign. Jeez, Tess, when did you become so impossible?"

"When you walked away from the company, leaving Blake and me knee-deep in a mess." Tess wasn't trying to be difficult, just firm. Besides, what she was doing was good for the company and good for Jason.

He couldn't walk away from his responsibilities whenever the spirit moved him.

"Trust me, this is for the best. You need to grow up, Peter Pan, before you turn out like Dad."

"Wow," her brother said with a chuckle. "You're sure not pulling your punches today. Does your bad mood have anything to do with Blake no longer working there?"

"No," she said flatly, not wanting to discuss Blake. Jason wouldn't understand.

"I don't believe you," he said in a singsong voice. "But if it's any consolation, you're better off if he's gone. It was only a matter of time before he broke your heart. Blake's not the kind of guy who sticks with things, especially a romance. Sorry you had to find out the hard way. At least you weren't in love with him." After a couple of seconds, he asked, "Tessie, you weren't in love with him, right?"

Tess sat up straight in her chair. "You know, you have a really low opinion of your best friend."

"I'm realistic. Blake's not the commitment type."

Deep down, Tess knew Jason was wrong. Blake was a good guy, a great guy. A man who believed in taking care of his family. Maybe all the responsibility he'd carried over the years made him leery of making any more commitments to other people, but he was still the best man she'd ever met.

"So, Tess, you didn't fall in love with Blake, did you?" he asked again.

Tess actually laughed. "What do you think?"

"Ah, hell. Want me to hunt him down and beat him up for you?"

"Of course not. You really are a sweet brother when you want to be—and when you're not disappearing on me."

"Thanks to you, I guess my disappearing days are behind me. Okay, here's the deal. I promise to come in to work first thing Monday morning all scrubbed up pretty. I'll be suitable for display to clients and employees both."

"There aren't many employees here to impress. Just Annie and Drew. Molly had her baby last week. You'll be happy to know he looks nothing like you."

Jason hooted a laugh. "It would be a miracle if he did."

Tess relaxed, feeling happy for the first time in a long time. She hadn't realized how much she'd missed her carefree brother until this moment.

"I'll be glad to see you," she admitted. "Even though you don't deserve me as a sister, I love you."

"Tess, I love you, too." He paused for a moment, then added, "I'm sorry if I've upset you. I guess I never thought it bothered you when I took off for a while. You never even blinked when Dad would take some time away."

"Well, now you know I hate it. You're being selfish, and I can't tell you how much I'm looking forward to you sticking like glue to this company."

"I'll do my best," he said, and Tess believed him. Her brother might not be perfect, but deep in his heart, he was a good guy. Flaws and all.

"When you try, Jason, your best is fairly good."

"Damned by faint praise. So, now that I've agreed to turn over a new leaf, what are you going to do about Blake? If you love him, you have to go after him. You don't want to spend the rest of your life miserable, do you?"

"Of course not."

"Well, does he know you love him?"

Good question. She thought Blake did, but she wasn't absolutely certain. They'd never talked about her feelings or his.

"I never said the words to him, but I think so," she said.

Jason made a tsking noise. "That's not good enough. Tell you what, when I get there on Monday, you head on over to Blake's office and tell him how you feel. That way, if you two decide you can't live without each other for a second longer and fly off to Vegas, I'll be around to manage the office while you're having fun in the city of sin."

Tess couldn't help laughing at his outrageousness. "Oh, right, and if Blake tells me to take a hike? What are you going to do then?"

"Then I'll show you what a true grown-up I've become, and I'll eat ice cream with you and hold your hand while you cry."

Should she really do this? Should she try again with Blake? Had she given up too easily? She wasn't certain. The only thing she knew for certain was that she'd never forgive herself if she didn't at least try.

Her decision made, she told Jason, "Okay, come

Monday morning, I expect to see your handsome face standing in my office. And then I'll do it. I'll go talk to Blake."

"Trust me, kiddo, you won't be sorry."

Tess could only hope that Jason was right.

BLAKE STUDIED Debra over her marble desk. She had a half amused, half surprised expression on her face.

"You're asking a lot, Blake. Don't get me wrong, part of me loves the idea, but you're in such a rush. I'm not sure we can pull it off in the time frame you want."

"Debra, I'm an expert at making minor miracles happen. If you say yes, I can pull it off."

Her expression was openly doubtful. She thought he was crazy. Who knew? Maybe she was right.

"Are you sure you're not setting yourself up to look like a fool?" Debra asked, toying with a pen on her desk. "I'm as romantic as the next person, but I can see all sorts of ways for this to blow up in your face."

Blake knew she was right. A thousand things, hell, more like a million things, could go wrong, starting with Tess telling him to get lost. But he had to try, and after the way he'd simply walked away from her, he needed to make a huge gesture so it was abundantly clear he was sincere. For that reason, he'd risk looking like a fool.

"I love her, Debra, and I certainly understand if you'd rather not get involved. But I think Loverboy could get a lot of good publicity out of this."

Debra gave him a long, contemplative look, and Blake found himself literally holding his breath while he waited for her answer. He wasn't doing this for Loverboy, but he also knew the cologne would get some terrific press if his idea worked.

All he cared about was Tess. If he told her he loved her, would she take him back? And if she didn't, what would he do then?

Refusing to even think about that possibility, he decided to push harder on Debra. "Haven't the ads worked? Aren't the sales what you expected?"

She raised one perfectly shaped brow. "You know Loverboy cologne is a hit thanks to the ads. Don't fish for compliments, Blake. I already feel like I owe you and Tess. My only concern is how this impacts Loverboy cologne if she says no."

Debra had a real point. If the press got hold of this and then Tess told him no, it wouldn't do much for Loverboy.

"It is a risk," he admitted, needing to be honest with Debra. Needing to be honest with himself.

"A risk you're willing to take?" she asked.

"Yes."

"I see. And what about your new partners at Markland and Jacobs? How will they feel if you end up making a fool of yourself? Can't be too good for business, and, I imagine, they'll be ticked off."

Blake shrugged. "I doubt it. I've already resigned. Things weren't working out the way I thought they would." He leaned forward in his chair, anxious for her decision. "I need to at least try. I can live with failing. I can't live with not trying."

By slow degrees, Debra's expression softened. Finally, she laughed. "Okay. I'm an idiot, but okay. I'm only doing this because I know she'll say yes. Then, you'll be back where you belong at D&S, and my company will be in good hands."

"Tess was taking care of your account. You were always in good hands."

Her smile was smug. "Yes, I was, wasn't I? Tess has turned out to be really savvy when it comes to advertising. I met with her last week, and she had some terrific ideas." She rested her chin in her palm and considered him. "But I really like the idea of the two of you working on my account again. This campaign was pure magic from the beginning. Think of what else you two can come up with."

"Exactly."

"So, we'll do this," she said. "And Loverboy can get great publicity out of this if it turns out well."

"Exactly. But if she turns me down, you can say that at least Loverboys are brave enough to go after what they want in life."

She drummed her long red nails on her desk, almost as if she were turning the idea over in her mind. "True. That sends a rather positive message, too. Well, either way, I'll help you, Blake. I just hope Tess knows what a lucky lady she is."

"I'm the lucky one, Debra," he told her, meaning it. "Tess is everything I want out of life."

With a laugh, Debra grabbed her phone. "Then let's get to work. Who am I to stand in the way of true love?"

"YOU AREN'T GOING to believe this," Annie said, bursting into Tess's office a little after seven on Monday morning. "I still can't believe it."

Tess rubbed her forehead, hoping the dull ache there would magically disappear. She'd been at the office since five, ostensibly to catch up on her paperwork, but she'd really arrived early because she couldn't sleep. She hadn't slept well in days. All she could think about was Blake.

As soon as Jason arrived, she was heading over to Blake's office to tell him she loved him. Deep down, she was scared spitless. She'd spent the night endlessly worrying about what he'd say.

Tess leaned back in her chair and looked at Annie. "What won't I believe? That Jason's back? I know he's coming in this morning."

Annie grinned. "He's already here. He's parking his car. But that's not what I'm talking about. You really didn't see it on your way to work this morning?"

"I drove in at five. It was pitch-black outside, so I didn't see a thing. So, what's the big deal?"

Annie's smile only grew. "Oh, no. I'm not telling you. You have to see this to believe it. Come with me." She moved around to Tess's side of the desk, and tugged her out of her chair. But Tess refused to leave her office.

"Annie, I have work to do. Plus, I need to talk to Jason. Can't this wait?" Tess didn't want to be rude, but this morning was the worst possible time for goofing around with Annie and Drew. She needed to get ready for her meeting with Blake. She needed to have her thoughts straight.

Jason poked his head in the doorway. "Has she seen it yet?" When Annie shook her head, he turned to Tess. "Hello, Tess. Good to see you. Now get off your duff and take a look at this."

Tess sighed, her exasperation level growing by leaps and bounds. "Jason, I don't have time for jokes. You and I need to talk." When he continued to simply grin at her, she added in frustration, "You know I have plans for later this morning."

Rather than looking contrite, Jason's grin only grew wider. "Trust me, Tessie, you need to see this."

Sighing, Tess realized there was no way anyone was going to listen to her until she played along with this game. "Fine. Show me whatever you want to show me so we can get back to work."

Jason and Annie only laughed, and when they all got to the lobby, Drew was waiting for them.

"This is going to be terrific," Annie said.

Tess decided they had all lost their minds. She expected this behavior from her brother, but not from Annie and Drew. But still she followed the three of them outside and down the street half a block. When Annie pointed to the billboard next to the fast-food restaurant, Tess groaned. They'd brought her out here for this?

"I saw it on my way in to work, and I couldn't believe it," Annie said, practically bouncing. "Who would've expected Blake to do something like that?"

Tess knew before looking that this billboard carried

the Loverboy ads. Herve's had been posted up there last week. She glanced up, expecting to see it. Then froze.

Blake. The billboard featured Blake. In a Loverboy ad.

Puzzled, Tess took a couple of steps closer. Like the other Loverboy billboards, on the left-hand side Blake wore jeans and a T-shirt. He looked gorgeous, but on the right-hand side, he was spiffed up in a tux and looked downright heartstopping. Tess felt her breath catch in her throat at the sight of him. The billboard had the usual Loverboy logo and the saying about any man being a Loverboy.

But the words in huge letters at the top were what made tears form in her eyes. The copy read: A True Loverboy Knows When He's Wrong.

Tess sucked in a tight breath. The last line read: Tess, I Love You. Will You Marry Me?

Tears rolled unchecked down her cheeks as she stared at the billboard. How had this happened? When had he decided he loved her?

She looked at Jason, who came over and draped his arm around her shoulders. "Looks like the boy has finally come to his senses. It's your move now, Tessie. Go get him."

It sounded like an excellent plan to her. Tess leaned up and gave her brother a kiss on the cheek. Then, with a wave at Annie and Drew, she sprinted back to her office, wanting to find Blake. Wanting to talk to him.

Oh my God. He really wanted to marry her?

Her fingers were shaking as she dialed his office, but

the woman who answered told her Blake wasn't there. Tess didn't bother trying any place else. Instinct told her where he was. She grabbed her purse and her keys and took off at a run, heading toward her car.

Heading toward Blake.

Getting across town to his apartment seemed to take forever, as did the elevator ride to his floor. Then finally, *finally,* she was at his door.

With a feeling of déjà vu settling over her, Tess rapped on the wooden door, tension coiling within her. Although the billboard made it clear he loved her and wanted to marry her, she couldn't help feeling anxious. She wanted to hear the words from him.

When he hadn't answered after a minute or so, she knocked again. Where was he? Surely he hadn't been so cruel as to arrange to have that billboard put up on a day when he was out of town.

Tess groaned and hung her head. The man drove her crazy. How could he do this to her? She needed to see him. Right now.

"Come on, come on, please be there," she muttered, knocking again. She was about to give it one last try when the door flew open, and she found herself confronted by a broad expanse of naked male chest.

"Hello, Tess," he said.

She started to pull back her hand before it made contact with his chest, then stopped. Giving him a little smile, she gave in to temptation and touched all that gorgeous tanned skin. Still holding his gaze, she trailed her fingers over the dark hair dusting his muscles, following the path until she dipped her fingertips under the waistband of his low-slung jeans.

"Hello, Blake."

"Glad I'm entertaining you," he said with a chuckle.

At his words, Tess pulled her attention away from his practically indecent appearance and looked at his face. His sinful black hair was mussed, attesting to the fact that she'd gotten him out of bed.

"I love you," she said simply.

Blake grinned and tugged her inside the apartment, shutting the door behind her. "I love you, too. Are you here for the reason I'm hoping you're here?"

As much as she wanted to throw herself into his arms and tell him that yes, she'd love to marry him, she first needed to understand why he'd changed his mind.

"I'm here because of the billboard," she confirmed.

Needing distance from him, she walked over and sat on one of the leather chairs. Just like that morning so many months ago, Blake flopped on the couch and smiled his devilish smile at her.

Tess glanced around the living room. "Did you pick up all the bras and thongs before I got here?" she teased.

Blake chuckled. "Feel free to leave your bra and panties on the floor if you want to."

There was a distinct possibility that would happen. But first, she had questions. "Why did you do the billboard? And how did you do it? Debra's going to freak."

"Debra helped me with the billboard. As to why I

did it, that's simple—because I'm sorry it's taken me so long to come to my senses. I've been in love with you for a long time, and I needed to show you how I felt. I was afraid you wouldn't believe me." His smile turned wicked. "You haven't always believed everything I've said. So I talked to Debra, told her my idea, and she agreed to help."

"I think it's wonderful."

"Well, you may not think so when every newspaper and TV station within a hundred miles decides we're romantic and wants to interview us."

Love filled her. She couldn't believe how lucky she was. "I don't care. I think it's romantic." Then she asked the question she really wanted him to answer. "Did you mean everything you said on the billboard?"

Blake got off the couch and walked over to stand in front of her. Once there, he gave her a sexy little smile, then dropped to one knee.

"Tess Denison, I love you. I adore you. I can't imagine my life without you. Will you marry me?"

Tess felt her breath catch in her throat. "Yes" was all she could manage to say.

But it was enough.

"WHAT WILL your mother think about us getting married? And your sister? Won't they be upset?" Tess asked much later. She sat next to Blake on his bed, leaning against the headboard, eating the scrambled eggs they'd made a few minutes ago. It was late, after ten at night, and this was the first chance they'd had to talk.

This morning, after she'd accepted his proposal, he'd scooped her into his arms and brought her in here.

And made mind-blowing love to her for hours.

She snuggled deeper into the fluffy bathrobe she'd borrowed and looked questioningly at him.

"My mom and Lisa are thrilled," he said after he polished off the last of his food and set his plate on the bedside table. "They know all about my plan. In fact, a lot of this was their idea. Mom in particular thought I was a fool for letting you go in the first place."

"Good. I want them to be happy."

"Tess, you do realize they'll always be a big part of my life? Even after we're married, I'll still want to help them out. I've promised to put Lisa through college, although she's agreed to live at home with Mom while she's in school to cut expenses. She also wants to get a part-time job. But that won't pay enough for her to afford college on her own. She'll still need me."

"Of course she will," Tess said. "And hey, I have the perfect job for her. Molly only wants to work half days when she returns from maternity leave. Lisa can work the other hours."

"Sounds great, but her college tuition still costs me a lot of money each year."

"Money won't be a problem, right, because you make a lot at your new job."

Blake's expression was sheepish. "About that. I used to think being a partner at Markland and Jacobs would be great." He tugged on the belt on the bathrobe she wore but it remained knotted. "The truth is, I hate that job."

"Why?" The word came out as a squeak when he slipped one hand under the edge of the robe and let his fingers wander.

"I miss you. I miss D&S Advertising." He continued his exploration, and showed every intention of distracting them from their talk. But Tess wanted her questions answered, so, reluctantly, she tapped him on the shoulder.

"Hold off for a sec. I can't concentrate when you do that."

Blake chuckled, looking happier than Tess had ever seen him look before. "I'd hate to think you can balance your checkbook in your mind while I'm making love to you."

"Hardly. I can't even think straight when you're making love to me." She set her plate on the nightstand next to the bed. Then she ran her fingers through his hair, ruffling it and making him look sexy and adorable. "So, you miss D&S? Want your old job back?"

Blake kissed her long and hard. "Yes."

"I haven't had a chance to tell you, but Jason's back."

"Great." He kissed her forehead, the caress tender.

"And the good news is I've found three new clients. Plus, Drew, Annie and I just finished the first set of ads for Countrywide CPAs."

"Sounds terrific." He fiddled with the belt on her robe again until he finally got it untied. "And we shouldn't need to go after capital. Jeff Markland is going to contract work out to our agency. With all that, we should be in pretty good shape."

After helping her out of her robe, he shucked off the

boxers he'd put on before they'd cooked dinner. Once naked, he climbed back into bed, gathering her close. "I've missed you so much. And I really do love you, Tess. I never thought I'd want to get married, have a family. But I want all those things with you. You mean everything to me."

Tears formed in Tess's eyes. "I love you, too. I can't tell you how happy you've made me."

Blake gave her a sweet smile. "I want to spend my life making you happy."

This time when he kissed her, it was full of passion and love, promises and dreams. When the kiss finally ended, Tess nudged him with her elbow. She'd had enough talking. She wanted some action.

She gave him a mock frown. "Hey, Loverboy, considering how crazy we are about each other, don't you think it's about time you make love to me again?"

Blake grinned. "Sweetheart, it will be my pleasure."

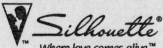

Harlequin invites you to walk down the aisle . . .

To honor our year long celebration of weddings, we are offering an exciting opportunity for you to own the Harlequin Bride Doll. Handcrafted in fine bisque porcelain, the wedding doll is dressed for her wedding day in a cream satin gown accented by lace trim. She carries an exquisite traditional bridal bouquet and wears a cathedral-length dotted Swiss veil. Embroidered flowers cascade down her lace overskirt to the scalloped hemline; underneath all is a multi-layered crinoline.

Join us in our celebration of weddings by sending away for your own Harlequin Bride Doll. This doll regularly retails for $74.95 U.S./approx. $108.68 CDN. One doll per household. Requests must be received no later than June 30, 2001. Offer good while quantities of gifts last. Please allow 6-8 weeks for delivery. Offer good in the U.S. and Canada only. Become part of this exciting offer!

Simply complete the order form and mail to:
"A Walk Down the Aisle"

IN U.S.A	IN CANADA
P.O. Box 9057	P.O. Box 622
3010 Walden Ave.	Fort Erie, Ontario
Buffalo, NY 14240-9057	L2A 5X3

Enclosed are eight (8) proofs of purchase found on the last page of every specially marked Harlequin series book and $3.75 check or money order (for postage and handling). Please send my Harlequin Bride Doll to:

Name (PLEASE PRINT)

Address _____ Apt. #

City _____ State/Prov. _____ Zip/Postal Code

Account # (if applicable)   **098 KIK DAEW**

HARLEQUIN®
Makes any time special®

Visit us at www.eHarlequin.com

A Walk Down the Aisle
Free Bride Doll Offer
One Proof-of-Purchase

PHWDAPOP

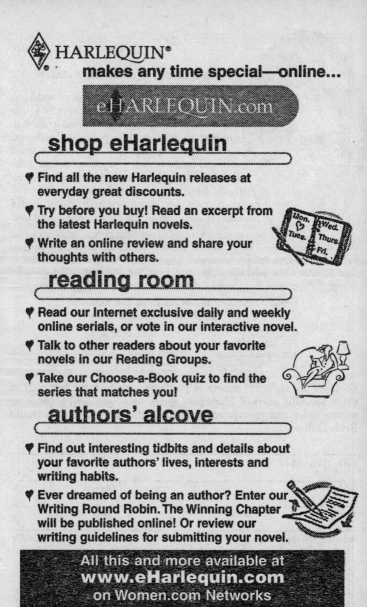

INDULGE IN A QUIET MOMENT
WITH HARLEQUIN

Get a FREE

Quiet Moments
Bath
Spa

with just two proofs of purchase from
any of our four special collector's editions in May.

Harlequin® is sure to make your time special this Mother's Day
with four special collector's editions featuring a short story
PLUS a complete novel packaged together in one volume!

Collection #1 Intrigue abounds in a collection featuring *New York Times*
bestselling author Barbara Delinsky and Kelsey Roberts.

Collection #2 Relationships? Weddings? Children? = *New York Times*
bestselling author Debbie Macomber and Tara Taylor Quinn
at their best!

Collection #3 Escape to the past with *New York Times* bestselling author
Heather Graham and Gayle Wilson.

Collection #4 Go West! With *New York Times* bestselling author
Joan Johnston and Vicki Lewis Thompson!

Plus Special Consumer Campaign!
Each of these four collector's editions will feature a
"FREE QUIET MOMENTS BATH SPA" offer.
See inside book in May for details.

Only from

HARLEQUIN®
Makes any time special ®

Don't miss out! Look for this exciting promotion on sale in May 2001,
at your favorite retail outlet.